AF255857

ANIMAL NOIR

CONTENTS

ANIMAL NOIR

ANIMAL NOIR

For everypony, I think

A NOTE FROM THE EDITOR

This was the most collaborative project I've worked on since I was a makeup artist. It had been so long, I almost wondered if I'd find something as magical as a brainstorming session for a script or hashing out scene blocking again.

The authors who helped make this book a reality brought that magic. They brought the sparkle and shine and silky fur and polished talons and fluffed feathers.

This was supposed to be something else, I thought—it was planned to be, at least. But soon after the authors and I started talking about vibes and world-building, I realized it was always supposed to be this. And I feel so very lucky that I was able to collect these voices for such a unique anthology.

I hope you enjoy New Growl through the years as much as we all do. Not all of the animals spend their time there, but like many of our most famous cities, there are connections everywhere.

—Elizabeth Mitchell

TWO SIDES OF THE TRUTH

ELAD HABER

Psst. Can you keep a secret?
I saw her, that older bird, talking to one of the servant pups. They
were being very familiar. Very friendly. You know what that means,
right?

The footpup produced a handkerchief from his breast pocket
and held it to her, his eyes downcast and his head bowed.

"This heat is murder, mum," he said in his puppy drawl.

Valeria, a Purple-Backed Starling of advanced age (but you
wouldn't know it), picked up the beige piece of cloth and dabbed
at her forehead. "I wouldn't know anything about that," she said
and handed it back to him. "Thank you for your kindness...."
She let the question hang in the air like a secret.

"Argus," said the footpup.

He was young, of course. They all were, in his position.
When he got older, he would move on to another function in the
house. Something less strenuous on the hips. Dogs were not
built to stand all day.

Argus' pose and outstretched paw were perfection, a testa-
ment to his training. Valeria used Argus' right paw to lower
herself into the backseat of the car. Another footpup appeared
to close the door and stayed standing while Argus stepped into
the passenger side door. The car had a curtained divider, so
Valeria had the illusion of being alone in the back, but she was
comforted by the presence of the driver and Argus, in case any
rough animals decided to waylay the vehicle.

There was a time when such concerns were not warranted in New Growl. One could walk down any alley at any time of day or night without fear. Nowadays, though, the world is different. The world is dangerous. And fear had infected every element of the city, from the upper class to the lowly servants and the cocksure criminals that slithered and skulked in the shadows.

Valeria fanned herself with a sensu, obtained on a recent trip to Asia. Cats done up with thick geisha makeup and kimonos adored a fan. Some posed provocatively, with their skirts hiked or showing half a shoulder. One particular bold feline licked her own paw.

Valeria didn't mind cats. Or dogs. In fact, she respected all animals who could appreciate her beauty. As usual, she wore one of her "stunning" dresses (that word had been used, verbatim, in an article about her). It was mint green adorned with tiny glittering diamonds, the front low, showing off her bosom, and backless, her brilliant purple plumage pushing out of her dress as if ready to scream. Her hair was dyed black for the occasion, makeup thick with color, her beak polished like the most expensive china.

There was a party tonight. There was one almost every night, despite the sorry state of the city and its bespoke crime. The city's noble class would not let petty concerns stop their fun. And besides, what would the newspapers print tomorrow if not the latest gossip? It was a service they were providing. A show. Money spent at the parties filtered down to the dressmakers, the chefs of the city, the liquor distributors. It was all very altruistic.

Although, in truth, Valeria (after a significant amount of drink) might admit that she is getting tired of this life. So many parties in so many mansions, they all blend together as if she never actually leaves the party. It just pauses and then starts up again somewhere else. The drinks are always the same, the animals the same, perhaps with some minor reconfiguration.

 TWO SIDES OF THE TRUTH

Some couples like to change it up and go to parties with someone else's partner.

There are whispers that those are just pretexts for other swaps that happen behind closed doors, but Valeria is never invited. She sometimes hears of after-parties in discreet locations. As if the formal party she goes to is just a precursor for the real gathering of the most elite.

That infuriates Valeria. She should be in the innermost of any inner circle. While she is not as young as she used to be (aren't we all?), she was once referred to—*again*, in an article—as the "most beautiful bird in the world." In fact, Valeria still keeps that clipping near her at all times. She mounted the gray newsprint on a piece of thick vellum, shaded pink, with gold trim. She would show it to you, if you asked.

She was once the star of any party she went to. Shuffled around to make sure she met everyone by the host. The one everyone looked at while they spoke in their tiny circles. Valeria was above all the small talk that took up the air in the room. She was a show bird. She was meant to be seen, not ignored.

All her husbands had been wealthy birds. They adored her, showered her with gifts of homes and vacations. She misses some of them. She shuffles a portion of her wealth and time to charity, but not much. Her house, her servants, take up most of her time and money.

And, of course, the parties.

The car was barely moving through the city streets. Valeria was just about to question the driver when he slid open the curtain a bit to apologize for the delay, blaming all this "traffic" on "some grubby animal protest in the Bellows." This was a new concept to Valeria. Traffic. Her servants drove her around, so she didn't know where most things were in the city.

The day had turned to night, and the omnipresent hustle and bustle of the city was changing, voyaging from a business day to a mysterious night. By the time Valeria's car arrived at the main entrance of the house, the sun was gone, and the world was a muted blue. Her footpup rushed outside to open her door and help her up. Argus looked like he had another comment saved up, but a look from Valeria quieted him.

The party was hosted in one of the newer brownstones that have been built in formerly poor neighborhoods. A chance for the *Nuevo* rich to show off their achievements. Valeria didn't mind. It saved her the trouble of hosting herself.

The door to the brownstone had a gothic affectation; twin gargoyles held the door in place in the midst of what looked like a battle, clenched fists and tails that looked like they would come alive from the stone and lash at her.

Valeria took a long look at the street below, doubts grasping at her heart, as if the door closing behind her was somehow permanent.

I saw something, too!
I saw her disappear into one of the bathrooms. I don't think she was alone.

The parties had taken on a more layered approach these last few months. Someone threw a "themed" party, a strained appeal to "pretend like you're in Paris" or some such nonsense, and the party throwers took it from there.

Tonight's theme is "Masquerade," but it appears to be rather low effort. Across from the front door are two large vases with masks attached to small sticks. Valeria took her time choosing one. The artifice of a bird pretending to be another animal of lower worth was not appealing to her. Everyone knew birds were the best of the world's creatures. She let out an audible sigh and settled on a poodle—a small white one with whiskers.

   TWO SIDES OF THE TRUTH

Valeria placed the mask on the bridge of her nose and strode into the party. The grand living room was crowded with animals.

Most of them held their masks at their sides like an afterthought, a few had one covering their faces. Valeria spotted a few masks facedown on a side table with a drink forgotten on top. So much for the theme.

She spotted the host of the party and decided to play along for the time being. She tightened the poodle mask a little on her face and approached the Barristers, the couple who owned the house—a charming but aloof pair of egrets with their thin arms locked. The husband had a habit of staring, as most husbands did.

"Woof," she said as way of greeting.

Mrs. Barrister burst into laughter. She gripped Valeria's arm. "Thank you for playing along, dear." She unlocked herself from her husband and led Valeria further into the house. "Have you been here before? No? Well, then, you must have the tour!"

Yes, of course. The tour. Valeria usually sneaks away during the inevitable slow walk through the house, but today she's right in the middle of it. No escape for her. There's always some grand reveal in the tour. Some new household improvement, perhaps a new piece of art or sculpture or simply "the view." She liked to guess what it would be as the hostess led her and a few hanger-on's through the house and up to the second floor.

"We just put in a new window in our bedroom," swooned Mrs. Barrister to her guests. "You can see the whole park from there!"

So there it is. The gaggle of guests walked up to the window and obliged with an "ooo" or "aww" sound to relay themselves properly impressed. It was soon Valeria's turn. She glanced out of the window. It was true, the view of the park was nice, trees as far as she could see, but her attention shifted to something closer, down below in a courtyard at the back of the house. She could see a number of animals huddled together as if playing a game out of sight of their employers.

They were all footpups in their tight-fitted outfits, their tails showing. One of them, a tall dark-haired pup, noticed Valeria and shouted something. She couldn't quite make it out. She did a kind of exaggerated wave and then turned away, showing off her namesake purple plumage. There was a bit of applause from the courtyard below and then something loud, followed by shouts.

"What was that!" exclaimed someone behind her.

Suddenly the window was crowded with others peering below.

"Was that a gunshot?"

"What happened!"

Mrs. Barrister spun on her heel and rushed out of the room. Valeria was right behind her. Normally, she wouldn't get involved in something like this. But her servants were down there, and if they were at all involved, well, she was part of it now too.

No one ever goes to her house. Apparently, all her servants are male. That's what they say.

The party was frozen in place as if someone had paused the world. Huddles of animals stood flushed to the wall, their drinks clutched but unconsumed. Conversation was halted, pending further information. The cheap masks were neglected on the floor.

Mrs. Barrister, with Valeria and the tour goers behind them, rushed into the grand room, full of sound and fury. Even their clothes shouted their arrival, rustling and scraping across the polished floor. The lady of the house shifted her narrow head around the space, looking for insight.

 TWO SIDES OF THE TRUTH

A door slammed open, and a group of servants came in carrying a body. The form was alive, whimpering and moaning. "It's one of the footpups, mum! He's been poisoned!" Poisoned?

Valeria felt glances fall on her. There were whispers she couldn't make out, and she resisted the urge to follow their source.

The servants carried him to one of the neatly adorned tables and dropped him on platters of aperitifs. Valeria strained to get a good luck at him between the crush of bodies. Fearful, she took a few steps forward. *Argus,* she thought. *Please don't be Argus.*

Someone moved, and she got a good look at the dark-haired pup who had shouted at her.

Mrs. Barrister was clearly flummoxed. "We heard some shouting and thought someone had been shot."

One of the servants, a thin ape with bulbous cheeks, shook his head. "No gunshot, mum. We were all playing a game when we noticed this one—" He motioned to the footpup on the table. "—on the floor and gagging. Look at his coloring. Something inside of him is wrong."

Everyone strained to look. It was true. His fur was taking on a lighter tinge, color fading from his face. His moans suddenly became hacking coughs. Spittle launched out of his mouth, and his limbs danced as if he was possessed. And then, he stopped. Collapsed into himself in such a sudden and decisive manner, it was no question what had happened.

The thin ape touched the pup's neck and reached for his arm to feel for a pulse. He shook his head.

"He's dead."

You heard what happened to her husbands?
All of them, poisoned.

Always get a second opinion.

They say that about medical diagnoses, but it's also right about the truth. Never trust the first version of events. It's rarely the whole story.

For example, Valeria's quiet car ride to the party tonight. What you heard earlier was not exactly true.

The traffic was atrocious, and Valeria was bored. She asked the young pup to move to the back with her.

"You have family in the city?" Valeria inquired of Argus.

Argus shook his head.

His eyes darted from the roof of the car to the seat and then back again. He didn't know where to look. Should he look directly at her? That would be disrespectful. But she's talking to him. Him looking away *is* disrespectful. But if he looks at her, his eyes might travel downwards across the curve of her beak, down the sinew path of her neck, and to the most interesting curves he's ever seen in his life.

No, it would be better to look away. And then he remembered she had asked him a question.

"No, mum," he muttered. "All my litter are out west, on the farms."

"Pity," said Valeria as she stared out the window. "It sounds so sad, being alone in a big city."

Argus could feel the sadness around his mistress and wanted to cheer her up. "Oh, I don't feel lonely at all. I have made many friends in the house. We're all quite happy."

Valeria allowed herself a smile at his enthusiasm, but then she sighed. "If only..." She didn't complete her thought.

Argus leaned forward, sniffed at the air with his snout. "Is there anything I can do for you, mum?"

Valeria extended one of her long limbs and gripped his thigh. "Actually..."

The ripple of rumor spread quickly through the party.

Valeria kept close to Mrs. Barrister and watched as she
became more and more distraught at this disruption of her
party, when in fact this tragic turn of events would be all the talk
for weeks if not months to come. She held the Mrs.' hand as if it
was one of her own children lying there on the table, squishing
the buffet.

Meanwhile, they whispered.

Someone said they saw the deceased footpup conversing
with Valeria earlier in the evening. Someone else spotted them
entering a bathroom together.

Partygoers nodded. That made sense, they told each other. It
wasn't the first time Valeria had been involved in a poisoning.

Gasps.

It's true, they whispered, their voices taut, their eyes darting
around to make sure only certain people could hear. She had
been known to take a lover, and when she was done with them,
they ended up poisoned. *Do you know how many husbands she's
had?* Ask around. Everyone knows. She even picked up a nick-
name, although no one would ever say it to her face.

What is it? What is it? they pleaded.

Venomous Valeria.

She likes her husband rich. And her servants young.
That's what I heard, anyway.

The partygoers continued to congregate in the great room.
Perhaps some ancient animal intuition to stay near watering
holes and avoid predators. All of the guests' servants were
brought in from outside and taken to a room near the kitchen.

Valeria stood alone, but within earshot of the hosts of the party. Mr. Barrister finally decided to rejoin the party from wherever he had escaped to. They spoke in whispers. She heard the Mr. recommend calling the constables, but the Mrs. shook her head. Something about a scandal.

Valeria cleared her throat. Sidled a bit closer to them. "She's right," Valeria said at a half-whisper. "You don't want a scandal at your *first* major society party. People may think it's unsafe to come to *this* part of town." She enunciated with purpose.

The Mrs. clutched at the pearls on her chest (really). "We can't have that. You have to help us, dear. What do we do?"

Valeria wrinkled her nose in thought for a moment and then said, "I'll be right back."

She broke away from the huddle and moved towards the kitchen. She felt the eyes of the party on her.

The small sitting room beside the kitchen was crowded with servants. They all hushed when she opened the door. Valeria scanned the room and locked eyes with Argus. He moved towards her, a wave of whispers in his wake.

"Come on," she said, and they exited the room together.

I never trusted her. No, too pretty. Too flighty.

"I'm scared, mum," said the nervous footpup as soon as the door closed behind them.

Valeria touched his arm, aware of eyes on them. "Don't—"

"But what if—"

"Shh," she hushed him. "Come with me."

Valeria veered Argus away from the guests and through a series of hallways around the grand living room. Whispers chittered from the sides of the room like nighttime cicadas.

They found an unoccupied sitting room. The closing door echoed in the sudden silence of the party. Everyone strained to

　　　　TWO SIDES OF THE TRUTH

listen. A few people walked by the door, their steps slowing as they crossed it.

No sound emerged.

As if afraid of waking a baby, the party guests moved towards the door to catch a whisper, a cry, a moan, any hint of the mystery beyond the door.

After a few long minutes, the doors fanned open. Valeria and her footpup emerged and escaped in different directions.

Some animals demand attention. She's the worst of them.

There was something else we didn't tell you.

Another encounter between Valeria and the footpup. It was a few days ago, late at night when the house was asleep. Valeria will sometimes wander her house (the top floors anyway) in a shift dress, slight and see-through, with only a wineglass as company. A tall and dark form emerged, and Valeria shrieked. Argus, standing, woke and shook his head, his eyes full of questions.

He started stammering something. "I'm sorry. I sleepwalk. I always—"

"What did you say?" Valeria interrupted.

"I said—" panted out Argus. "I'm sorry, mum. I always sleep-walk in new houses."

Valeria crossed her arms to cover herself. "You shouldn't be up here."

"I'm sorry," he said again, and went to leave.

"Wait," she said. She pointed to a nearby couch. "You should sit down."

Argus didn't argue. He collapsed onto the couch. He wiped his nose with his paw, then sat himself upright. Valeria sat next to him. He was wearing a white t-shirt and pajama pants, some puffs of fur showing. She moved closer and closer to him until their thighs were grazing.

*Does she have any friends? Anyone who knows **intimate** details?*

Amidst the gossip spreading like hors d'oeuvres, another door opened, near the kitchen, containing the gathered servants. They fanned out towards the buffet tables.

The lord and lady of the house rushed to the servants, demanding to know where they were going, what they were doing.

The servants were a wide selection of animals, usually subservient species. Yet they dressed in finery and acted more regal than even the highest noble. In a word, they had *class*, despite their social status.

So when one white-haired canine with glasses over his massive nose spoke with authority, they all listened.

"He was one of our own. We will take care of this."

A group of the other servants were already gathered around the dead pup. As if they were removing the main course, they leaned in, picked him up, and proceeded to funeral march him out of the house.

The Barristers said nothing. The party guests were enthralled, watching the play happen. When the door closed and the last servant exited, all the guests seemed to relax and moved towards a loose gaggle in the center of the grand room. The whispers became exultations.

Between you and me, I don't trust any animal with wings.

Later, Valeria emerged from a side door to the back patio. The electric lights were on, and she followed a trail to the detached servant's quarters. She knocked on the simple door.

     TWO SIDES OF THE TRUTH

There was a hush from beyond the door, and it opened just a crack. It was Argus, waiting. He motioned her in.

They were crowded in there, the servants just as curious to the night's events as the party guests and the newspaper readers tomorrow morning.

Valeria nodded at the crowd, then turned to Argus.

"How is he?"

"Grateful, mum," said Argus. "With the money he earned tonight, he can venture back home to see his wife and newborn."

"And the potion?"

"I destroyed the rest of it just like you told me to."

"Good." Valeria turned to the watching animals. "And all of you, I hope we can count on your discretion."

They nodded and smiled.

Argus made a kind of grunting sound. His eyes darted to all sides as if bracing for an attack.

Valeria trained her eyes on him. "You have concerns?"

"No, mum. I have no reputation to uphold. But I worry..." He got out that last part painfully, as if speaking from the heart for the first time. As if the truth was something simple that can be told, instead of a multi-faceted crystal that changes based on the angle of the onlooker.

"I worry about you," he said, finally looking at her. "You have a name and friends here. They're already gossiping about you. And tomorrow, with the papers, they'll be so much talk."

Valeria simply smiled. "Isn't it glorious?"

OUR SONG

BETH COOK

By Beth Cook

"Witness testimony, August 30th, 1926, New Growl. Please state your name and species for the record." The local boar officer, Higgs, waves vaguely to the doe typist in the corner taking down every word.

I clear my throat. "John Latif. Leopard gecko."

"Ha! John, huh? Not Abu Mohammed Al-Something?"

"Just... John." My father's family fled to England when he was young, and he insisted on his children having English names. Nowadays, as nation after nation was declaring independence and ousting the English from their ancestral homelands, my father doubled down. English names, dress, schools, jobs. *They will always see us as other, my son, but at least they will see us as safe.*

The British mastiff, Detective Williams, sits head and shoulders taller than me. The case is now serious enough that Scotland Yard sent him on the week-long journey across the pond. "Thank you, John. Can you tell us if you were at Fluffner Hall on August 19th?"

"Yes. That is, *partly*. My employer had me running errands that morning."

"Mr. ... Ruvido Wingley? Can you identify your employer in these photographs?"

The first shows a teenage kingfisher, stiff and stone-faced in the uniform of some boarding school for the daughters of lords. The next shows the Ruvido I know, a slightly older kingfisher, jacket slung over a chair and shirtsleeves rolled up, cheeks puffed out mid trumpet-blare.

"Yes, that's him."

Williams nods. "Legal name Lady Rosemary Wingley." He

slides the photos back into his files. "Mr. Latif, do you believe your employer had any particular grudge against the late Lord Fergus Fluffner?"

"Oh, he—sorry, 'late'?" I suppress the urge to lick my eyeballs and blink hard instead. *We must never seem too reptilian when surrounded by mammals.*

Higgs slurps his coffee. "Oh, didn't you hear? Guy turned up fried to a crisp." He tosses another photograph onto the table. A twisted, blackened body. Flesh burned away down to a permanently screaming lagomorph skull.

"Wingley blames the whole thing on a ghost," sneers Higgs. "But ghosts don't start fires, bub. We want the facts."

Williams pours me a glass of water. "Let's start back at the beginning."

I arrived at Fluffner Hall in mid-May. I'd been hired by Ruvido's father, Old Lord Wingley, as his son's personal assistant and business secretary. His father was reluctantly willing to reintroduce Ruvido to society as Young Lord Wingley *if* he could manage to keep out of mischief. I thought that's what I'd signed up for—a straightforward business relationship with a spoiled rich kid staying with family friends for the summer.

The door opened, and a disheveled kingfisher in a loose robe blinked at me. "Oh, right, that's today."

"Well, howdy!" His flushed companion, a saucer-eyed toad with an American drawl, waved.

Ruvido and Melody led me through the enormous house, stepping over loose music sheets, empty wine bottles, and a snoring tiger with a tuba pulled down over his eyes.

"Officially, it still belongs to the Fluffners. Lady Fantasia, the last Fluffner resident, was an unmarried eccentric and general disappointment to the family," Ruvido said with admiration. "When the Bohemian wave hit, she converted her ancestral home into a music hall and opened its doors to famous maestros and penniless strummers alike."

Melody took a short blonde wig off a bust of Mozart and pulled it onto her bald amphibian head. "Fantasia died in 1886, but the residents here have sorta... permanent squatters' rights. Maybe you'll even get to meet her some day," she added with a wink.

"Ah ha!" A wild-haired, round-bellied red squirrel hopped onto the bannister of the grand staircase, slid all the way down, and was suddenly inches from my face and shaking my hand.

"Cornelius Walnuttington at your service, Master of Ceremonies at Fluffner Hall, and president of the Order of Visionary Devotees to Revitalize Audiophilia."

Ruvido laughed at my stunned expression. "Cousin Corny, this is my new business secretary, John Something."

"Latif, sir. Pleased to meet you."

"Welcome to Fluffner Hall, Mr. Latif! My family's been organizing concerts here for generations."

I later learned that at some point, the employer-employee lines were crossed and made the Walnuttingtons technically family, if only with begrudging acknowledgement from the Fluffners.

"Which reminds me—Ruvido, Melody, I've just received word that the New Growl chapter will be joining us this summer! Now that we've had the whole place fully modernized and electrified," said Cornelius, "they're bringing all sorts of incredible new recording equipment. It'll be the reunion of the century!" Cornelius turned back to me. "Tell me, young man," he said with a waggle of his enormous red eyebrows. "Do you like jazz?"

Snap! I flinch as the memory of my forbidden jazz records breaking in my uncle's furious hands brings me back to the present.

"Mr. Latif, did you ever meet someone named Calliope Scherzo, alias 'The Feral Diva'?"

Oh.

Shit, don't hesitate. "Yes, sir." I try to remember Ruvido's coaching. *"How to cooperate with a police investigation without ratting anyone out."* "She made an appearance at the New Growlers' jazz exhibition."

"And was that the only time you encountered Ms. Scherzo?"

Damn. How to lie without lying? Everyone staying at Fluffner Hall knew the Feral Diva was Cousin Corny in a huge red wig, makeup, and gown. To the outside world, he was merely a harmless eccentric.

"It was the only time I spoke with her personally. She was one of many notable guests."

"What did you speak about?"

"Just standard introductions." Yes, she introduced herself. She also introduced me to the soul-igniting miracle of live jazz, marijuana, eyeliner...

"And when did you first meet the late Lord Fergus Fluffner?"

"The following week, sir, upon his arrival at Fluffner Hall." The sneering, sniveling worm of a mad hare in a pencil mustache and a wardrobe of plaid suits that conveyed all money and no taste.

"Did you ever witness any animosity between Lord Fluffner and Ms. Scherzo?"

Besides the countless arguments, passive-aggressive notes, and drunken threats between distant cousins who hate each other but are forced to play nice in public? "Detective, I do not wish to speak ill of the dead, but Lord Fluffner had a remarkable talent for inspiring animosity in everyone.”

Williams asked more about Fluffner’s time at the hall, and I stuck to the facts, leaving the rest unspoken. “He wrote to announce his arrival the following week as the new owner of Fluffner Hall.”

His father had let Cornelius stay and run things according to Lady Fantasia’s wishes, but upon his father’s death, Fluffner arrived to claim his inheritance and return it to a seat of British nobility. “He brought in new staff from his own estate.”

Alfie, the ancient rabbit butler, was the only paid servant left from the old days, and in the decades since, the hall had adopted a merry anarchy with all residents contributing to its upkeep. When Fluffner dismissed Alfie, Corny promptly hired him back as a singer. But we saw how frightened Fluffner’s own staff were of his wrath and retaliation. In reintroducing the hard lines between Upstairs and Downstairs, Fluffner hoped to end dozens of inter-class parties, friendships, and love affairs, though really they just moved to the servants’ quarters.

“He spoke of his great plans for the future of Fluffner Hall.” He threatened to turn the recording studio into a bulletproof steel vault, the auditorium into a textiles factory, and the gardens into a zoo for those of us whose species were not native to Britain.

Detective Williams shuffles through his notes. “Did you have any interactions with him on the day of the fire?”

“We crossed paths in the early evening. He asked where the Feral Diva was, and I said I had no idea.” I’d been humming and dancing through the hall like a blissed-out fool when Fluffner appeared and shook me by the collar, demanding to know where she was. When he finally believed I was useless, he let me go. I sat on the stairs holding my arms and face to the heavens to bask in the music that might have been my friends practicing in the next room or might have been all in my head. "I didn't see him again until the concert began, when he ran in and grabbed the music sheets, shouting that he was going to burn every trace of music, and the next thing we knew, the whole place was ablaze."

"Anything else you remember about that night?"

"Not much, unfortunately." Because I was out of my gourd on reefer and German wine. "When the auditorium filled with smoke, I fainted. I woke up on the lawn with the others who'd escaped and carried me to safety. We could only watch in horror and wait for the fire brigade."

"Mr. Latif, we've interviewed dozens of witnesses. Half of them blame the deceased, and the other half blame a ghost. What do *you* believe?"

"I'm afraid I can't think of anyone else who could have done such a thing." In the crackling flames, I could swear I heard Fluffner's maniacal laughter, followed by a ghostly wail.

The Mirror Maze is everything wrong with New Growl. Identical towering buildings lined with one-way glass so that everyone inside can see you, but you are not allowed to see them. Every day I walk in the rain beneath towers of cold steel, lifeless concrete, glass with all its colors drained away and all its shapes beaten into flat submission.

At least Fluffner Hall was in lush, green countryside with blooming gardens. Even my tiny London flat was in a colorful immigrant neighborhood, families crammed together in public housing with cousins and neighbors everywhere, always some Auntie or other making sure I was fed.

Here, I am alone. After the fire at Fluffner Hall, some went to London, some to Paris, and I joined Ruvido and Melody with a handful of musicians on a boat to New Growl. Ruvido and Melody barely leave their suite at the Purrchester Hotel, and I haven't heard from any of the New Growler musicians since we arrived. Perhaps the bonds I thought I'd made at Fluffner Hall had never been real friendships, just proximity and tolerance. Have I ever been able to tell the difference?

"Tss. *Oye*, gecko." A soft voice.

I whip around, looking for the source.

"Over here. The alley."

I follow the sound into a narrow, dark space between two buildings. No mirror glass here, just service entrances and trash bins. And a figure in the shadows with two tiny, bright eyes darting around in different directions.

"Who are you?"

"They call me the Chameleon. Listen, you're getting caught up in something dangerous. Something big. Fluffner saw you that night."

"How do you know about Fluffner? Were you—?"

"*You* were just yapping to the coppers." It wasn't a question.

"I... no, I promise. Mr. Wingley coached me on—"

A bitter laugh. "*Han gled in på en räksmörgås*. Rich creatures always think their money's gonna keep them safe 'cause it usually does. But not this time. The hawks are circling, and sooner or later they're gonna figure out what happened."

"But what *did* happen? If Fluffner didn't accidentally kill himself, then..." I feel my stomach drop into my shoes. "They're trying to pin it on Corny, aren't they?"

"He's the next in line to inherit Fluffner Hall, so of course it looks bad. No one has seen or heard from Corny or the Feral Diva since that night. The most popular underground radio show in England suddenly went dark. Everyone knew Fluffner and Corny hated each other, so what better scapegoat?"

"But if Corny's innocent, then surely the evidence will prove it?"

"*Ay, dios mio,*" they mutter, "*Urwać się z choinki?*" A small, tired sigh. "Look, it's adorable that you think playing it safe will *keep* you safe. Just keep your eyes open and your trap shut."

They flick a card at me, and I fumble with my umbrella to catch it. On one side, only a spiraling green C. On the other side, a hastily written clue: "*Little Silk Road—where the corn god plays the jade flute.*"

When I look up, I'm alone again, except for the lingering scent of something warm, floral, and spiced.

The next day, I steel my nerves to demand some answers from Ruvido, but when he lets me into their suite, my prepared speech leaves my brain entirely. The place is a mess of clothes, sheet music, records, and liquor bottles as the couple rushes about, packing their bags.

"What—what's happening?"

Ruvido shoves a crumpled telegram into my claws.

RABBIT BODY IDENTIFIED AS FOOTMAN ALFRED LONG-SHANKS STOP FLUFFNER STILL AT LARGE STOP TRUST NO ONE BUT THE ORDER AND GET OUT OF NEW GROWL STOP

—TFD

My claws shake, but my voice comes out surprisingly steady. "You did do it. All of you. You set the fire and tried to kill Fluffner, and now he's out for revenge."

"No, no, you don't understand!" Ruvido rushes over and, instead of shaking me by the collar like Fluffner did, he only wraps his hands around mine and looks right into my eyes, desperately earnest. "No one was supposed to die, John. Not even Fergus, as much as we all joked about it. But especially no one innocent like Alfie." He chokes on the name and tears begin to flow. He clutches my hands tighter. "We only tried... We only wanted Fergus to *understand*, so he might give up his stupid crusade and..." He chokes up again.

"Remember, Ruvy." Melody, wearing at least a dozen necklaces, looks up from sorting through her various wigs. "Plausible deniability."

Ruvido steadies himself and lets go of my hands. "Right. Sorry, old sport, but it's best that you don't know any more, so you can answer honestly if you have to. But I promise you, none of us started that fire intentionally."

"So then why leave?" With a sudden flutter of hope, I add, "Oh, please tell me we're going back to England."

Ruvido shakes his head and resumes his frantic pacing. "I can't. My father called on the telephone this morning, all the way from England. He found out I'm wanted for questioning and demanded I come home and say Corny did it. He'll only accept me as a man if I'm *his* kind of man." He shuffles through a pile of records, and I get the feeling he's not really reading the labels. "When I refused, he cut me off. Emptied my accounts. All I've got is some cash and whatever possessions I can carry. Not even my stupid title."

Melody drops her bag and toad-hops over the settee to gently hold her lover's face. "Babe, we don't need none of that. Remember, I grew up in a shack with a dirt floor, singin' with the crickets and dancin' with the fireflies. We're gonna be just fine. We got *us*."

I turn my face away from the intimate moment, aching and anchorless.

Melody comes over and hands me a velvet box.

"Here. We got two boat tickets outta here, but there ain't enough cash for a third. Maybe you can sell this?"

Inside the box is a stunning ring, a flower made of pink, purple, and green gemstones. I snap the box shut and pocket it with a short sigh. I'm alone, but at least not entirely destitute.

"And here." Ruvido hands me a record. "You should have a copy."

"Our Song" by the Feral Diva Calliope Scherzo and the International Order of Visionary Devotees to Revitalize Audiophilia

"But... how—?"

Ruvido shakes his head and winks. "Plausible deniability, old boy."

I pack my traveling cases, check out of the splendid Purrchester, and step out into the rain again. With each hand carrying a heavy case, I cannot hold my umbrella open, so I resign myself to getting drenched. I've never set foot in my ancestors' desert homeland, but something in my bones still yearns for it.

There's only one place I can imagine going. I follow the concierge's directions to the Little Silk Road neighborhood.

I hear the bazaar first, and then smell it, before I ever see it. At last I turn a corner, and it's like I'm back to my own London neighborhood. An open city square packed with food stalls, colorful awnings keeping off the rain, flags and prosperity figurines and bowls of sweets, a pod of musicians drumming and singing in a language I don't recognize, and creatures from every continent. It's more colors, smells, and sounds in one city block than I've experienced in the last four months combined.

Mealworm vindaloo for lunch renews my courage, and I begin looking for the Chameleon's clues.

At last, there he is, what can only be the corn god, painted on the side of a Mezoamerican food stall. I spin around, and there's the jade flute, painted on the sign of a Chinese tea stall. I back up slowly, pivoting this way and that, until the two images connect and it looks like the corn god is playing the jade flute.

At my back is a wall of hanging fabrics in Slavic prints. I peek between two sheets and step into a tenement housing courtyard—colorful murals and painted fire escapes, potted plants, and chicken coops. Clotheslines hung with laundry, flags, and baskets to send goodies back and forth between neighbors. Next to a lush community garden, children splash barefoot in the puddles, babbling in a mashup of who knows how many languages.

Sitting in a folding chair next to the curtained entrance, a snoring walrus with a huge, bristly mustache snorts awake and notices me. "Hey, hmph, hey. Who's this?"

I show him the Chameleon's card, and he narrows his eyes at me for an unnervingly long stare-down. "Fifth floor, east side, mango tree door."

When I find the door painted with a mango tree and set down my cases, before I can knock, I hear a voice from inside getting louder. "*Órale*, Marco, if I find out you took the last arepa again, I swear to *la Virgen*—"

The door flies open, and there they are. I do not know if a chameleon can blush, but I see their skin shift through several vibrant color patterns before settling back into soft greens and blues. We stare at each other for what feels like an eternity, yet is over too soon. They relax into a lopsided smirk. "Took you long enough."

Carmina. Their name is Carmina.

When I tell them I haven't seen or spoken to any of the musicians who came back with Ruvido, Melody, and me on the boat from England, they grab my cases and say, "Well, we're gonna fix that."

I change into dry clothes, and when we meet back in the courtyard, Carmina has changed from their plain shirt and trousers into a silvery flapper dress and cloche hat. If I wasn't obviously stuck on them before, there's no denying it now.

They bring me to the Blue Grove neighborhood and the Cottontail Club. Among the house band are the musicians I traveled with—Harper, Piper, Hook, and Allegra—who seem genuinely delighted to see me, and we all catch up during their break.

When the music turns from snazzy to sultry, Carmina leads me onto the dance floor. That warm smell—jasmine, sandalwood, and cardamom. They fit in my arms perfectly. And I am utterly gone.

For weeks, Carmina and I barely leave their room except to go back to the Cottontail Club nearly every night. We get to witness Louis Wingstrong, Cab Cassowary, and Duke Shellington. As we dance, I can feel the music being etched permanently into my heart like a wax master disc in a recording studio.

Whenever I bring up Fluffner Hall or the investigation, Carmina evades my questions like the master shapeshifter they are, but I cannot bring myself to care. The more they reawaken my frozen senses and buried longings, the less I want to go home.

One afternoon, as we're lounging in the park, I feel a shadow loom over me and block the sun. When I sit up, I'm face to face with Detective Williams.

The picnic blanket next to me is suddenly empty. I know Carmina can't be far away, probably blending in with a tree or mural, but I can't blame them for hiding. The longer they can keep their name and face out of this investigation, the better.

I play innocent, that I merely moved hotels and neglected to tell anyone at the precinct because I assumed they were done with my small, unimportant testimony. But Williams plays the politeness card right back, sitting down across from me to ask "just a few more questions."

I try not to gulp visibly. "Of course."

"There's just this matter of your whereabouts on the morning of the fire. You said you were out running errands at these locations?" He shows me a notebook with the shops and offices I went to that day.

"That's right."

"Strange. You see, there's a new witness, one Madam Fifi, who Lord Fluffner brought in that day to, quote, 'exorcise the ghost of Fantasia Fluffner,'" he says with well-controlled sarcastic skepticism. "She claims she saw you several times that morning, as you answered the door and escorted her into Fluffner Hall."

I have no words, and Williams lets me stew in my confusion, watching me closely. When I returned from my errands that afternoon, the folks at Fluffner Hall told me all about Madam Fifi's short-lived visit—she ended up siding with "the ghost" and refusing Fergus' money—and I had forgotten about her since.

"Detective, I can honestly tell you that I never saw the woman."

"Mm. And there's no chance you could have forgotten such an encounter? Perhaps from being, say, intoxicated?"

"No, sir." I didn't have a sip or a puff until after teatime, like a proper British gentleman embracing Bohemian hedonism.

"Mm, good. One hears so much about artists and the various substances they consume, legal and otherwise. I'm glad no one at Fluffner Hall lured you into such debauchery."

A polite nod and smile. No lure was needed, I'd been like a fish willingly jumping into the boat. "Perhaps this hired medium was... confused."

God, I hope she's old as well as eccentric. I don't want to throw some woman I've never met under the train, but what else can I conclude?

"Perhaps. She did say the leopard gecko had a thick New Growl Accent, which you decidedly do not."

I promise Detective Williams that if he has any further questions, he can call for me at the Little Silk Road post office (close enough for convenience, anonymous enough that he won't be able to find Carmina's place).

When he leaves, Carmina materializes out of the bushes. They settle into anonymous solid green, pull their flat cap over their eyes, and say, "Let's go home."

I wait until we're sitting side by side on the edge of their bed. "I'm pretty sure I would remember if there had been another leopard gecko in Fluffner Hall. But there was a chameleon. Someone I only saw from afar and wasn't there very long, so I never got to know them." I shake my head, laughing at my own absurd notion. "But even a chameleon who mimicked the color pattern of a leopard gecko would still look like a chameleon."

A deep breath beside me. "Unless the creature they needed to fool was a racist blue blood who thinks all lizards look alike."

I nod slowly. "It was you."

Carmina does not look at me. I watch their hands clench and unclench, over and over. "We were smuggling out the records, and someone had to distract Fluffner. So I volunteered to be the loud, noticeable one answering the front door while Corny snuck out the back."

"So... why use me as your disguise?"

Clench, unclench, clench. "I don't know. I'm sorry, I really don't. I'd seen you around but never worked up the nerve to talk to you. If I had, if we'd have become friends, I never would've done it. I just... had you on my mind, I guess. I needed to be someone else, and I picked the nearest thing I could believably become." They groan and start balling up the fabric of their trousers in their hands. "Ugh, and then I kept talking about how I'd just seen the Feral Diva in the front hall so Fluffner wouldn't go snooping around back, and..."

"And that's why he thought I knew where she was. Well, there's one minor mystery solved."

The radio, always left on to some local station or another, faded into a new song.

My head snapped up. "Is this...? It can't be. Wait, no, it definitely is!"

Carmina nods. "We made dozens of copies. Smuggled them out and sent them in every direction. I got a copy to our local station, and they've been playing it more and more. I guess people like it."

"It's... gosh, it's as beautiful as I remember."

'Our Song.' I take Carmina's hand, squeeze and release, squeeze and release. We lean our heads together and just listen. The energy picks up toward the end of the song, and I hear a familiar tinkle. "That's me on the tambourine."

Carmina smiles. "Do you remember that day?"

"Oh, you mean my first mushroom trip and communing with a ghost?"

"Wait, *what*? You saw Fantasia?"

I shrug. "Or something. I thought it was the drugs, but when I told Ruvido and Melody that I thought I'd seen a blue, transparent, singing Great Dane, they said it was her. I somehow knew she was a Great Dane without ever having seen a picture of her."

"Ohhh, that's probably what gave them the idea! I heard them talking about how if they could just get Fergus to do psychedelics once, it would 'expand his mind' and he'd 'talk to Fantasia' and 'learn to love music' and... I thought it was ridiculous until..."

I slapped my hand to my forehead. "Until the night of the fire! They *drugged* him! That's why he was acting so wild and paranoid."

Carmina sighs. "Some people get high and realize we're all universally connected, and others just become even more convinced of their own power-hungry delusions." The final quiet *ting!* of the song, and Carmina grins. "That's me on the triangle."

"You were there too? Incredible." We snuggle closer. "Dozens of creatures crammed into a recording studio—some of us still tripping on mushrooms!—all playing one incredible song that couldn't have existed without us."

My heart aches, thinking of sweet, quiet Alfie dying for a rich kid's prank. But at the same time, what a gift to have this song preserved forever. I don't know if any song can be worth dying for, but in this moment, it feels worth it to keep living for.

Carmina lights up with a sudden thought. "Have you heard the secret B-side?"

It's supposed to be the day of the 40th Annual Fantasia Fluffner Memorial Concert. Carmina and I meet up with the Cottontail Club musicians, wondering if the Feral Diva will manage to still pull it off somehow.

We step out into the stormy evening, and I tell Carmina I'll meet them at home. I head toward the post office to check for a telegram from Corny, just in case. I walk along the street next to the river, feeling every rumble of thunder shake the ground.

A flash of lightning, and a horrible, leering face appears inches from mine. They grab me and hurl me to the ground. We tussle, they get in a good punch, and I taste blood.

I can make out two long ears on the figure pinning me down. Another lightning flash, and I see him clearly.

Fergus Fluffner has found me at last.

"You!" he hisses, grinning feverishly. "Where is she? Where is she?!"

"Here I am, my darlings!"

Fergus startles, looking around and seeing nothing but the radio in the drugstore window. I spit out blood and smile. The secret B-side.

"Ladies, gentlemen, and wild animals of every kind, the Feral Diva is back!"

"No-no-no-no-no," Fluffner whispers.

"My name is Calliope Scherzo, and I host a little underground radio show in England. But for the past several weeks, listening audiences around the world, from San Francisco to Istanbul, have been hearing the thrilling new song brought to you by the International Order of Visionary Devotees to Revitalize Audiophilia."

Fluffner scrambles away from me, hissing, "She's here. She's everywhere!"

"Tonight, on this 24th of September, we bring you a once-in-a-lifetime event—the 40th Annual Fantasia Fluffner Memorial Concert—live, from everywhere! I want every last one of you, wherever you are in the world, to sing and dance and play along with us. We named this song not just for the musicians who first wrote it, but for all of you, all of us, everyone around the world. This is 'Our Song.'"

The music begins, and Fluffner watches in horror as the

ordinary people of New Growl flood the streets, dancing and singing in the storm.

"John!" Suddenly Carmina is at my side, holding me tight.

In the next flash of lightning, I see a long-eared figure running, the pitch of his scream in perfect harmony with the music.

I sit up, wipe the blood off my mouth, and pull a little box from my pocket. Carmina's eyes widen as they see the jeweled flower inside. "What do you think, love? Sell it for two boat tickets out of here, or call it an engagement ring?"

They throw their arms around my neck, laughing and crying and kissing me.

Ting! goes the triangle.

The crowd cheers and keeps dancing in the rain.

FEMME PRÉDATRICE

A.P. HOWELL

FEMME PRÉDATRICE

By A.P. Howell

Barbara paused at the frosted glass window of the third floor office. Reasonably well-painted block letters spelled out JOSEPH DONOVAN PRIVATE INVESTIGATIONS, but she could still see the remains of a previous tenant's name, the letters almost but not entirely scraped away. Appropriate for this city, constantly reinventing itself, but never quite forgetting what had come before, never quite managing to create something better.

The previous tenant had been an attorney, apparently. Barbara wondered what sort of law he—almost undoubtedly *he* —practiced in a run down third floor office. She grimaced and knocked. An educated socialite of means should not be consulting *any* professional in this sort of office.

"Let yourself in," a voice called from within. She took a moment to smooth back her spines before opening the door. "What can I do for you, Miss—?" The mongoose behind the desk set down a file and gestured for her to sit.

The available chair was wooden and looked very much second-hand. Someone with a bit of skill and pride in his possessions could have refinished it into something decent-looking. But it was, at least, a chair that could accommodate a range of body types.

The mongoose was flanked by filing cabinets which had seen better days. Barbara wondered how many of them had belonged to the erstwhile attorney, or perhaps an even earlier tenant. Containers of take out food balanced precariously in an over-full trash can.

"Anderson. Barbara Anderson, she/her, *Atelerix sclateri*."

The snout wrinkled a bit, in mild amusement. "Joseph

Donovan." He gestured toward the door that bore his name. "He/him, *Urva edwardsii.*"

He was older than her by perhaps a decade—a hard decade. His muzzle was grizzled, prematurely silvered fur mixed with natural gray. One ear was missing a small chunk, and his snout was scarred with scratches; she suspected there were more such scars under the cheap suit. He would have been a soldier, young but not a child, gone away to war and then dropped back into his old city, to find the citizenry made alien by his own experiences.

"I must confess, Mr. Donovan, that I never expected to find myself in this position." She paused and visibly suppressed fidgeting fingers.

"Take your time, Miss Anderson. But the more you tell me, the easier it'll be to get you into a more comfortable position."

An old charm lingering in the voice. It had probably been a nicer voice, once, but it had taken on a smoker's rasp. The remains of a cigarette sat in an ash tray in need of emptying, the smoke curling ceilingward. The entire room smelled of cigarettes—his, the attorney's, and years and years of clients'.

"I have lived in many places," Barbara said. "I have the means to go where I like."

"And you liked Oxbridge."

She nodded, unsurprised that he had noted her accent. "Though obviously, one does not attend the university without family support."

"Was it a university, or was it a finishing school? In your particular case."

Barbara felt her gaze go cold. "Is there a difference between universities and finishing schools? Real life is not about tutors—whether that real life consists of the practice of law or medicine or politics or philanthropy or household management."

The mongoose, who she knew held a professional license

but no academic qualifications beyond a pre-war high school diploma, offered a conciliatory shrug.

"I recently found myself in need of a change of scenery," Barbara continued. "A past romantic entanglement made life... uncomfortable."

"What was the nature of the entanglement?"

"Nothing so sordid as your normal business, I suspect. It was... not quite an engagement, but there were expectations on both sides."

The mongoose nodded, looking as though he suspected the situation was, in fact, sordid. Good. Embarrassment was an easy explanation for providing thin details.

"Our families were close. There were expectations, but he failed to meet mine. I didn't bear him any particular ill-will. We were both young, and if it turned out that we were a poor match, how much better to discover that *before* a wedding?"

She sighed, not longingly, but with the premature world-weariness of heartbreak.

"You didn't bear him any ill-will," the mongoose prompted. "Past tense?"

"I am being followed," Barbara said. "I don't know who he is. I don't recognize him—he's a cobra."

"Ah," the mongoose said sourly. "I think you misunderstand the nature of my business."

She allowed a horrified look to cross her face. "I want you to find out who he is and who he is working for. And if there are any others," she added. "Oxbridge doesn't train one to spot tails or anything of that nature. For all I know, there may be more men following me."

"You think he was hired by your almost-fiancé?"

"Perhaps. Perhaps his family. Or..." She paused and looked downward, the picture of misery and shame. "Perhaps my own family."

"Do you feel as though you're in danger?" he asked. "Or is this more of an embarrassment?"

"It is most definitely an embarrassment." She pulled herself upright. Her body might not lend itself to physical intimidation, but she put steel in her voice. "Please understand that this is not merely a matter of bruised feelings. Business interests may be harmed by even a hint of scandal. Hence my choice to approach you, rather than the police. I value discretion."

He nodded in acknowledgement. "If this man was going to turn violent, I suspect he'd have made a move by now."

"Probably so." Barbara allowed a hint of unease to creep into her voice.

"But you're not sure."

"I haven't spoken to… him since I made the break. Nothing I know about him suggests violent intent—but I have misjudged him in the past."

"I don't suppose you would be willing to supply me with the name of the almost-fiancé? Address, contact information? And his family members? And yours, for that matter," the mongoose said. "In case they take you for a little girl lost."

Barbara grimaced. "They are overseas. If you can avoid involving them…"

"No need to worry. I wasn't planning to ring them up and ask if they'd hired someone to investigate you."

They shared a smile.

"Shall we discuss my rates?"

Barbara pulled out a checkbook, then paused with a pen hovering above the ivory paper. "I suppose cash is preferable?"

"Works for me."

Cash spent anywhere, with no delays before deposits cleared and no paper trail for the tax man. Not that Donovan was a habitual tax cheat; it was more reflex than philosophy.

He didn't often get high-class clients, but they trickled in sometimes. It was usually divorce cases, people who didn't want to risk rumors spreading within their own circle. Their bills—like Barbara Anderson's—were usually crisp. Swallowing their judgmental looks was part of the job.

On balance, Barbara Anderson hadn't been very judgmental. Perhaps her recent embarrassment had instilled a bit of empathy—not something native to the Oxbridge set, in his limited experience. He fished a bottle and cleanish glass out of the bottom drawer. She'd been on the lookout for booze, and Donovan was faintly gratified that she hadn't seen it. Conforming to the stereotype of an alcoholic veteran P.I. was bad enough; broadcasting it to clients was another thing entirely.

As he drank, he considered the stalker. If you wanted muscle, you wouldn't hire a cobra. They had two modes: non-violent and venom. (A constrictor, now, there was a snake who could cause degrees of pain. Most folks, slowly suffocating, would agree to pay their debts and whatever new vig was imposed. No marks afterward, either.) The cobra in question would've been hired for other skills, presumably investigative.

Donovan didn't know of any cobra P.I.s in the city, but that wasn't surprising. Posh clients didn't call from away to hire local talent; they sent their own guy.

The out-of-town guy had to stay somewhere, and normally Donovan would've asked around. But it was tough, being a mongoose asking about cobras. Lot of ugly history there.

Donovan's reputation was as an investigator, not muscle (the old leg wound twinged at the thought). But he didn't need to raise any eyebrows by asking around about an out-of-town cobra. Keeping an eye on Barbara would be the best way to find the cobra following her.

She wasn't so young, was she? Old enough for Oxbridge University (however much of a degree she'd finished—her reaction to the finishing school comment made him think she hadn't focused too much on classwork), old enough for a familially-approved marriage—and, presumably, old enough to access whatever trust fund she was living off. Younger, but not *young*.

He wasn't so old, was he? Even if forty was closer than thirty. He might not be a prize, but he was working, and he'd come out of the war less scathed than so many others. Older, but not *old*.

He scrawled her name on a fresh folder and pulled out a pile of newspapers, flipping back through the society pages. It didn't take long to find her. She didn't warrant a lot of mentions—this town had plenty of socialites, including the homegrown set—but her name did appear on guest lists. There were a few photographs, too. They were grainy, and Barbara Anderson was rarely the main subject, but she was recognizable.

She looked good in all the photos. Knew how to dress for formal occasions: cute, ingenue-type looks, jewelry that caught the eye but didn't go overboard. Just the right amount of white belly fur visible above the bodice. Her fur was dark, in sharp contrast to the white fur of her face around the dark snout.

Classic *Atelerix sclateri*, subtly different from other hedgehogs —it was mostly *Atelerix albiventris* in the city, in the world—who tended toward lighter brown fur and paler spines. (Except some of the younger set, who dyed themselves all sorts of colors. Weird thing to do, given the imperfect color vision of most folks, including hedgehogs. But what did he know? He wasn't young.) You couldn't really tell in the black-and-white photos, but in person, her coloration, including the blonde-tipped spines, was obvious. (To him, anyway. His color vision was excellent.)

Donovan went to work with his scissors. Couldn't afford a

clipping service, and anyway, this was more discreet. A case like this, finding out about the client was the easiest way to track down the animal harassing them. *She* might only be able to think of a handful of possible culprits, but there could be others. The young and the rich could be terribly careless.

Not just rich, but posh. You might be able to get a checking account at the Deosai Bank just based on the size of the deposit. But you didn't get into Oxbridge without connections. You didn't get invited to the right parties without connections.

Atelerix sclateri. She'd been born into an exclusive group. Regardless of cosmopolitan gestures toward species equality, it still mattered. The old guard would come out and say it. The youngsters folded it into their introductions, as though species (or at least genus) was not otherwise obvious, or a detail weighing neither more nor less than name and gender.

Donovan sighed. Barbara Anderson made him feel old. And she made him want to feel young.

Barbara sank into her bath.

The claw-footed tub was her favorite feature of the apartment. It was big, comfortable, and classy. The apartment itself was small—appropriate for a woman living alone—and classy-adjacent. She wasn't ashamed of her address. It also wasn't quite worth broadcasting.

But the current apartment had served her well over the past several months, not least because it had been available and furnished. It would be a good place to hibernate. The bedroom window was small and non-drafty.

Hibernation was a double-edged sword. On the one hand, it reduced expenses and the chance that society might grow weary of one's presence. Let them ask, "Oh, when will Barbara join us again?"

On the other, one still needed to pay rent, and there was always the chance that society might forget one's existence. For a socialite, "Barbara who?" was an unbearable prospect.

Only days ago, she had been in the society pages. She had sparkled at the party, conversed with local movers and well-known out-of-towners and more than a few foreign guests. She had a stack of invitations to upcoming events, issued to her in her own right, and a few requests to be a plus-one at even more exclusive events.

Barbara Anderson was *not* going to give all that up just because of a stalker.

The cobra tailed her to a salon, and the mongoose followed.

It wasn't a particularly upmarket place, let alone trendy. Maybe she was changing up her routine, knowing she was being followed. Otherwise, there might be a favored cosmetologist or source of gossip, or else he'd seriously misjudged, and she was short of funds.

The cobra was pretty good at blending, checking out a magazine stand with plausible interest. Donovan was pretty sure the cobra hadn't spotted him. This city was his home turf; he knew the angles of buildings, where the shadows fell, and the patterns of foot traffic to fall into or avoid.

The salon had big windows, advertising of a sort. The salon workers—and, Donovan knew, owner—were all sika deer, but the clientele was pretty diverse. Several were getting mani-pedis, apparently enjoying the process of other people cutting their cuticles and scraping under their nails. (Donovan shuddered. Even thinking about that sort of poking and prodding brought back memories of the field hospital.)

Barbara was skipping the pedicure, apparently, keeping her shoes on but still getting her fingernails done. (Or touched up: her manicure had looked quite professional in his office.) She was also getting her spines dyed. Maybe the blonde color wasn't natural. (It had been convincing.)

The snake had a camera. Donovan hadn't noticed at first; it was under his cape, hanging from around his neck. Donovan was conscious of staring, watching the cobra twist his body, use his head and hood to manipulate the camera and take a shot. It was a small model, expensive, designed for use without paws or digits. Levers and big buttons essentially made it an assistive device, except the cobra's body was fully functional.

Pictures of Barbara—pictures of *his client*—should have been Donovan's primary concern. But for a moment, he was in the hospital again. Limping around with a crutch, being shown different exercises to strengthen damaged muscles, promised improvement if never again full functionality in the injured leg. He'd been too young to grasp the permanence of disability and too distracted by others' woes to wallow. Missing limbs, disfigured faces, wracking coughs, blindness, deafness, paralysis, head wounds that stole the ability to interact with the world, stole entire personalities and a lifetime of memories...

Donovan shook his head. The past was the past; he'd lived through it, built his life, and now he had a job to do.

He muffled the impulse to challenge the cobra. It wouldn't do any good, starting something in the middle of a busy street. Tailing Barbara's tail was still the best plan.

Getting spines dyed took forever, apparently. Donovan shifted uncomfortably from foot to foot and began thinking of his next meal. Hunger pangs during a stakeout wouldn't be a problem for the cobra, assuming he'd eaten in the past month.

And it wasn't particularly cold, so the cobra—sensibly bundled up—wouldn't tire quickly. Donovan's fast metabolism and four-chambered heart were not advantageous.

Was Barbara planning to hibernate?

If she wanted to sleep easy, Donovan would do his best to oblige. Find out what was up with the cobra and whoever had hired him. Maybe... maybe ask if she wanted to keep him on retainer. Just in case any other suspicious types rolled into town. Maybe it would make her feel a bit safer.

When Barbara finally (finally!) left, spines as blonde as before, the cobra took another picture. No window in the way this time, and even though the light was dim, Donovan thought he'd probably gotten a good angle, certainly good enough to identify the photograph's subject.

If the film was ever developed...

An out-of-towner was unlikely to have a darkroom in his hotel bathroom. He'd probably drop the film off to be developed, and Donovan was on good terms with a number of local photography techs. Exposing the film to a tragic amount of light might cost anywhere from a favor to a twenty.

The cobra followed Barbara, and Donovan followed the cobra. After it became apparent to Donovan that she was heading for her apartment, the cobra ducked down an alley. He slithered past refuse and between buildings, making his way toward Barbara's building with no chance of being seen from the street.

The cobra took his camera out again. From the mouth of his chosen alley, he'd have a good angle on the entrance to Barbara's building. Donovan heard him snap a series of shots, then fall silent.

Donovan peered around the corner. The cobra was looking up at the apartment building across the street. If he knew her building, it wasn't that surprising that he knew her apartment

 FEMME PRÉDATRICE

number. After a short wait, lights turned on in one of the apartments. The cobra snapped a couple more pictures, even though no hedgehog silhouettes appeared in the windows.

"I know you're there," the cobra said.

Donovan stepped into the alley, supremely annoyed with himself for getting clocked.

Mongoose and cobra: they found themselves in a cliché. The cobra had to be wondering, as Donovan had, if species had any impact on hiring.

"I'm not against sharing information," the cobra said. "But my client's got dibs on Wagner."

Wagner? The name hadn't been on Barbara's list, but Donovan kept the question out of his expression. Better to let the cobra talk.

"Not surprising she hit someone else," the cobra continued. "She spends money like a champ, but she's still socking some of it away. Can't tell if she's being stupid or smart. Strike while she's young and cute, hoard the proceeds for when her twat's shriveled up."

If Donovan hadn't been thinking a lot about Barbara's youth and cuteness, would he have kept his cool? If it hadn't been a cobra—a sleek, confident cobra with the funds for good equipment—would he have cared so much? Those questions nipped at the corners of Donovan's mind, as he found himself advancing down the alley.

The cobra hissed, low and threatening, almost a growl. His head snapped forward, closing the distance in an instant. A mongoose had nothing on a cobra when it came to reach. Old instincts surged up within Donovan, but too slow.

He was lucky. Instead of a bite, the cobra's lunge delivered a head-butt to Donovan's snout. He staggered backward, bloodied and disoriented. Now, the cobra unfurled his hood and drew himself up, much taller than Donovan.

"Time for you to leave," the cobra said.

And it was. He *knew* that. But it was one guy, unarmed (aside from the venom—but Donovan was a mongoose, he was tough). It wasn't a squad of soldiers. He was in an alley in his city, not an open, bloody field disfigured by trenches and barbed wire and noxious clouds. He hadn't been able to do any good there, no matter the medals he'd been given; but he could handle himself here.

Especially since the cobra didn't want a fight. Not really. Cobras were all about the quick strike. But he hadn't bitten. Donovan bared his teeth. Maybe he wouldn't have to visit photomats after all. Maybe he could take the film off the cobra right here—and take him down a peg or two.

Cobras were all about the quick strike, but a mongoose won through attrition. Dodge those strikes, dance around, tire the opponent. Donovan wasn't much for dancing anymore, not with his bad leg, and acrobatics were out of the question. Still, he circled, and when the cobra struck again, he dodged enough to take the punch with his shoulder, not his face.

He leapt forward and skittered sideways, clawing at the cobra's hood. Got behind him, scratching the back of the neck. The cobra didn't like that. Everybody's neck was vulnerable— but against a mongoose, the cobra's neck was *classically* vulnerable.

Fighting with a cobra in an alley wasn't the dumbest thing Donovan could've done—not as dumb as, say, following the cobra to an even tighter tunnel—but it was still pretty bad. He *knew* that, tactics running through his brain quickly, instinct and regular experience and the terrible, unnatural experience of wartime violence. But a fight wasn't just tactical advantage; it was about who wanted to win regardless of the odds. And right now, Donovan had that advantage—

And maybe the cobra picked up on that, some imperceptible

change in Donovan's expression, something primitive and bloodthirsty. Because there was fear in the cobra's expression. Donovan grinned with bloody teeth, feinted left—

—and the cobra struck, lightning-fast, fangs penetrating fabric and flesh and withdrawing before the pain registered. He'd never been bitten by a cobra, by any sort of snake. Shot. Gassed. Never bitten. They were all too damned civilized for that, most of the time.

The cobra backed up—straight back, toward the opposite wall, not the mouth of the alley. He wore a hard, wary look, waiting for Donovan to keel over. And that was Donovan's moment, leaping straight forward, no finesse, just throwing his weight at the cobra, bearing him back against the brick wall, clawing and biting down.

He'd never bitten a cobra. Too damned civilized, most of the time.

With a sigh, Barbara settled into her favorite chair. She waggled her fingers, the claws filed short, sharp, and glossy pink. Pink was cute, one of the staples of her wardrobe. Different shades were appropriate for different seasons. Now, as the weather grew chillier, her chosen shade reminded her of roses and sunny summer days. Days when she had *not* needed to worry about a cobra watching her every move.

One adapted to circumstances, found ways to navigate difficulties.

Barbara had grown up knowing the world had already been broken and remade. A woman could not simply count on marriage, a lifelong partnership and division of labor, or (even better) support. Not with so many men gone.

It was easy to forget, but hedgehogs were predators. She

could fight for what she wanted. But a husband seemed a sad goal, as likely to become a hindrance as support. Why constrain one's social circle and financial fate when one could instead embrace travel, independence, and excitement? A woman could move through the world unmarried.

She kicked off her shoes. They were... fine. Cute, even. A seasonally appropriate brown with pale pink accents. Barbara wouldn't have minded them so much if she could also wear open-toed shoes. Cute summer sandals, strappy heels for formal occasions...

She sighed again and wriggled her eight toes against the carpet.

Venom resistance. Something you knew from early on, and right after you were told about it an adult would stress how *resistance* wasn't *immunity*, how you absolutely did *not* want to be bitten (and why would you be bitten? Are we savages?) and if you were, you needed to get medical attention.

Good advice, if you were a poor innocent assaulted by some rando. But there was a dead man in the alley. Mongoose, cobra. It didn't look good. (It wasn't good.)

Donovan wasn't making good decisions. (He hadn't been making good decisions.) Instinct said to get away from the man (corpse) that had hurt him, get away from the place where he'd done something wrong (killed a man), find someplace that felt safe (...).

And so he'd lurched up the stairs—nicer than the stairwells in his office building—and down the hall, weaving, probably leaving blood on the walls, on the carpet. The camera dangled from his neck (theft), and he knocked on the door. The apartment the cobra had photographed. Barbara's apartment. His client. The closest maybe-sympathetic animal he knew.

He leaned against the door. Had the shakes, on top of the bad balance and nausea. Couldn't think what he was supposed to do—other than go to the hospital, but that choice was too far and too late and too fraught.

But Barbara might know. Hedgehogs were resistant to snake venom, too.

The door opened a couple of inches. He was slumped down, on eye level with Barbara. Her eyes widened, and after the barest hesitation—not even enough time for him to croak her name—closed the door again. The links of the chain rattled, and Barbara threw open the door for him.

Donovan made it three steps into the apartment before collapsing at her feet. Fuzzy slippers. Pink.

She lost one of the slippers stepping over him to close the door. "What happened?"

The words echoed in his skull. He knew they made sense, but it didn't seem important right now. The carpet was soft. He was bleeding on it, like he'd bled in the alley. But it was soft. Smelled better, too.

The pink slipper filled his vision and the bare foot. He blinked, counted twice because math was extraordinarily challenging, reached out with a paw. Four toes. Not five. Smooth, unmaimed skin. Four toes. *Atelerix albiventris.*

"Followed him," he said into the carpet. "Pictures... took pictures at the salon, your window." Could she understand what he was saying? Because he thought he understood her. Pygmy hedgehog. Common. Common as him, but she was young enough to want something better.

The camera's strap went over his head. "Were you *bitten*?"

She already had her arms around him, helping him upright and steering him deeper into her apartment. A bad memory welled up, being dragged along by another man in uniform, trailing altogether too much blood.

"Bitten." The word came out thickly. Blood in his mouth. Not all of it was his. "He's dead."

Barbara froze. "Dead?"

He thought he had nodded, or maybe it was just that she'd started moving again. A short hallway. Bedroom. No pictures on any walls. "Venom resistant. Like you."

The bed was made, a soft and fluffy pink comforter. Barbara tried to ease him down, but he dropped the last few inches. He sank, imagined for a moment that he was just going to continue sinking. Down, down, down forever.

The mattress springs caught him, pushed him skyward. He worried about blood, but she didn't seem to care about little details like that. The thought warmed him.

"You're like me." He closed his eyes. "It's okay... won't tell. Nobody's business."

"Poor thing," she said, the words empty of pity but filled with a compassion he'd happily spend a lifetime accepting.

Her paw stroked his forehead. Donovan hadn't felt this safe in years.

Then, she held a pillow over his face and pushed down.

The police officers were very solicitous, as was the detective. Barbara, recently tearful, sat on the living room couch. She remained the very picture of a woman suppressing horror. One of the officers made her a cup of tea, clearly uncomfortable with a woman's tears. She smiled gratefully at him and curled her toes deep into the soles of her shoes. No more accidents tonight.

The camera obviously belonged to the snake, whose involvement was implied by the bite. Before calling the police,

 FEMME PRÉDATRICE

Barbara had pulled out the film and held it up to the light. She doubted the cobra had photographed anything particularly incriminating, but it was better to be safe. She'd tossed the ruined film onto the shelf in her closet and replaced it with an empty roll.

"I know this guy," the detective said when he emerged from the bedroom.

The detective hadn't been in there long. Enough time to identify Donovan and look at his wounds, but not enough time to conduct a search of the room. He didn't sound particularly surprised that Donovan had died violently.

Given two corpses with matching bites, Barbara believed the police would draw the obvious conclusion and, hopefully, close two murder cases quickly.

It wouldn't take long to find the cobra's body—Donovan couldn't have walked very far in his condition—but it might take some time to identify him. Rifling Donovan's pockets, Barbara had found not only his wallet, but the cobra's. She shoved it under the mattress, where a dying man might have hidden them for reasons of his own.

The cobra was not local. The people who had presumably hired him—the people whose money, given willingly, albeit under false pretenses, had allowed Erin Wagner to become Barbara Anderson—would only know the trail of an *Atelerix albiventris* had gone cold. Or at least complicated, with their P.I. missing and, later, found to have died. Hopefully, they would give up, write off their financial losses, and move on with their lives. The rich could afford carelessness as easily as vindictiveness.

"What was your connection to the victim?" the detective asked.

It was something of a pity about Donovan. A chivalrous protector might have been worth the risk of someone knowing

Barbara Anderson's secret. But she did not think either chivalry or secret would have survived a murder investigation.

"I met him once, when I hired him. I was worried that someone was following me." A hint of tears. "I don't think he took me seriously. But I had some money, so he said he'd... said he'd help."

The best lies weren't lies at all.

Barbara wasn't common. She was exceptional, deserving of respect and luxury. She might not have been born *Atelerix sclateri*, might not have been born Barbara Anderson, but she could make Barbara Anderson true.

And she could defend herself, her true self, her new life. It was easy to forget, but hedgehogs were predators.

 FEMME PRÉDATRICE

AT THE EDGE OF
THE GUNMETAL SEA

M. SHEDRIC SIMPSON

By M. Shedric Simpson

I caught my first glimpse of Deirdre Nesbitt as I entered Beltham —a pale figure drifting along the bluff above the village, almost translucent against the salt-stained sky. I didn't recognize her, not then. Just took her for a portent of something terrible to come.

Worry tickled the scruff of my neck. Every sense told me I shouldn't have come. Shouldn't have taken the job in the first place. It wasn't my sort of work, and an alley cat like me had no place under such a vast and aching sky. But there're times when we all need to fight against our better instincts.

The fact of it was that I needed the money. Enough to get out of New Growl before the city chewed me up and swallowed me, the way it had so many others. So here I was, with a name on my tongue and a gun in my pocket.

A truck careened past—the Nesbitt's Fine Fish logo emblazoned on its side. I sent the borrowed Mewick Standard Six lurching toward the shoulder, but a cascade of gravel still pinged against the door panels. By the time the dust cleared, the ghost on the bluff was gone. I focused my eyes back on the road and told myself I'd imagined it.

Beltham wasn't much to look at. A cluster of old Victorians crowded the heart of the village—every one of them as bone-tired as I was after five hours of driving. Old shops with patched cedar shakes, their cast iron railings barely clinging to second story balconies.

The towering shape of the old cannery rose up on my right. A brooding block of wood and metal at odds with the rest of the village. Almost a century old, from what I'd dug up in my research. Peeling paint said the factory had seen better days.

Just like so many of us in New Growl, I'd grown up on Nesbitt's fish, and their tins had been a premium currency in the trenches. But the war had ended years ago, and folks wanted better now. Something fresh, instead of a reminder of rationing and air raids.

Nesbitt's was a name in decay, just like the village surrounding it.

I glanced at the map spread across the passenger seat. The estate stood to the north, perched between the village, the ocean, and the emptiness of the sprawling heath. Upon that same bluff where the ghostly figure had just vanished. I scrunched my whiskers and wove the Mewick past all those peering faces, every one of them telling me how much I didn't belong.

The buildings fell away, and a twisting lane led me up the west side of the hill. The gate stood open. But of course they knew I was coming. I'd sent the letter myself. I drove through, and Nesbitt Manor rose up above me.

Halfway between a temple and a mansion, the manor still emanated a kind of dignity that age hadn't managed to strip away. The central wing stood three stories tall, clad in pale pink stone. Ionic columns braced enormous balconies that overlooked the coast, and black iron finials decorated the roofline. Yet, for all the grandeur, an air of ruin hung over the place.

The lane ended in a loop some hundred feet in front of the house, with a closed-off drive leading around to the west. I pulled the Mewick over and stared up at that imposing facade. My whiskers twitched. I took a breath and forced them to settle.

Judging by the envelope of cash in my breast pocket, my client was already plenty rich. Yet his kind always wanted more. I swung the door open, and salt wind scraped my nostrils. Old money. Old blood. I should have known better than to get caught up in it. But I'd been born on the wrong side of the Growl, and there was a price to getting out. I'd pay it either way.

In the end, it always came down to blood.

The landscaping looked like a bad haircut—hedges ragged, roses escaping their trellises. A paved walkway marked the path to the door. The ascent had been designed to inspire awe, but only left me with a sense of pity. All this opulence fading—I could almost hear Father Time's hyena laughter.

I stopped at the front porch and tucked my tie inside my waistcoat. I was wearing my best suit while pretending it was my everyday. Dark grey cashmere over a pinstriped cotton shirt and a pair of polished leather Oxfur shoes. Not the latest style, but the guy I was pretending to be wouldn't keep up with Bright Water's latest, anyway.

The door opened before I could knock. Predatory green eyes locked onto mine, sharp and fierce. The fox's fur was the color of rust and burning houses. I couldn't shake the sense that she was looking down on me, even though I stood half a head taller.

"You'd be the banker," she said. Her teeth flashed in the afternoon light. Grey streaks gave her an aura of dignity, and her voice made me want to comply, even though she hadn't given any orders.

"Thomas Stray," I said. I showed her the card I'd made up. "Barklays Bank."

She looked me up and down, then gave a dismissive nod. "I'll take you to see the lady."

I'd fought under generals who were less imposing. "Ma'am," I said. I took my hat off as I stepped inside, then followed her through a maze of corridors.

More than what was there, my eye lingered on what was missing.

No paintings or tapestries, and half the furniture was missing—just discolored patches marked where the decor had once stood. The place looked like the third day of an estate sale at some moldering Willows Weep mansion.

"I'll ask you to keep from troubling the lady overly," the fox said. "Doctor's orders. If she's upset for any reason, I'll be escorting you out immediately."

I gave a little chirrup of assent, playing the acquiescent clerk. Three years in the infantry had given me plenty of practice at keeping my head down, and this visit was just to get the lay of the land.

All those hallways made the manor feel bigger on the inside than the outside—a labyrinth that was easier to fall into than escape. Eventually, the fox pointed me towards a doorway.

I gave her a polite nod and stepped into the office beyond. Brightly lit, but redolent of dust and old books. A massive oaken desk dominated the space. It must have been as old as the house itself. Behind it, a row of leaded glass windows offered an expansive view of the back patio and the gunmetal-blue sea beyond.

The room was well-kept but lived-in, with a tea service sitting on a cabinet to the right, and a stack of leather binders on the left side of the desk. At the center of all of it all sat the ghost from the bluff: Lady Deirdre Nesbitt herself, hunched over the blotter, with an accounting book opened in front of her. The woman I'd been hired to kill.

The curls in Deirdre's pale grey fur reminded me of waves on a pebble beach. And there was something childlike about her features—ears too big for her skull and wide blue eyes that filled

     AT THE EDGE OF THE GUNMETAL SEA

half her face—but the tragic gaze she gave me carried the weight of far more than her twenty-six years.

She wore a faded blue dress that must have been from the last century, with long loose sleeves and bits of lace gathered around the bodice. Finely made, but even I could see the wear along the cuffs and collar. The scent of mothballs drifted off her like a fine perfume, though she seemed oblivious to the smell.

Old nobility for sure. Devon rex or some other blue-blooded feline lineage. Nothing like the shorthaired domestics I'd grown up around—most of us hadn't even known our parents.

I pulled out a business card, crisp and cloud-white, with the bank's logo painted in the corner. I'd forged it myself, because sometimes paper opens doors more easily than steel. "Thomas Stray. I'm here to review the books."

"Of course," Deidre said. "I'm sure you'll find them in order." She gestured to a chair across from her. "How far back do you want to start?"

She spoke with confidence, but her left ear twitched just the same. Maybe the condition the housekeeper had warned me about, or maybe just the stress of being audited. "This year's numbers will be fine," I told her.

Deidre nodded and shuffled through the stack of binders, then slid me a stack of nine. One for each month. "Care for tea?"

"Yes. Thank you." I was a coffee drinker myself, but Thomas Stray drank tea. And I didn't like having my back turned to that fox, so I was glad for the excuse to get her out of the room.

"Mrs. Reed, a fresh service, if you would." Deidre leaned back in her chair, then straightened, as if she wanted to relax but didn't know how.

I flipped the first binder open as the fox swept away the old tea serving and vanished into the hallways. Numbers swam in front of me, but it didn't take an accountant to see there was more red than black. The cannery had been fighting for its life, and the blood was spilled on these pages.

The second file looked much the same, and I had a suspicion it would be like that all the way back to the war. I made a little growl of consternation at the back of my throat.

"This is everything?"

Deirdre hesitated. "I did add some personal funds, but you'll see those noted at the end of the month."

"Personal funds?"

"Auctioning off some of my grandfather's collectibles. They were only gathering dust."

The picture started to come clear. She'd been emptying the house to keep the business afloat, but that would only carry her so far.

"I just thought the money would be more useful there—" Dishes clattered in the hall, and Deidre jerked upright, her wide blue eyes somehow growing even larger. A moment later, the fox appeared in the doorway with the tea service. Deidre's head sank back down. "Oh, yes. The tea. Thank you, Mrs. Reed."

"My lady, please. I'll take care of our guest, if you'd like to rest." She spoke to Deidre, but glared at me the whole time.

"I'm fine," Deidre said, then turned her attention back to me. "Mrs. Reed worries I'm taking after my mother. Hereditary myopathy."

I'd heard of it—a wasting disease that plagued the upper classes. There was no cure, just slow decay until the heart suddenly stopped. A hard fate to bear. "I'm sorry about your mother."

Deidre rose, then stepped towards those great glass windows. "I was... an excitable child," she said. "Too much so for my mother. I wish I'd understood that when it still mattered. When it might have made a difference." She straightened, and her tail twitched under her dress. "I've learned to be better about such things, however."

I took a sip of the tea that Mrs. Reed had set in front of me. Black, with notes of bergamot, lavender, and chamomile.

The clink of porcelain sounded too loud in the little room.

"Is that her, in the green dress?"

She turned to her left, where a row of paintings hung along the wall. "Yes. I suppose she was my age at the time. I'd only just been born."

"And your father?" I nodded towards the portrait beside it.

"No, his brother. Uncle Kenneth."

I gazed up at the brooding eyes and mask-and-mantle coat of my client. Well, presumed client. The tom that had visited my office had been a sleek little tabby. Exactly the sort I would have asked out for a drink, if I hadn't known better than to mix work and pleasure. He'd barely said anything, just told me the name and told me to "get her out of the way." Then he'd handed me the envelope of cash, with a promise of double when the job was done.

I've learned not to take work when I don't know who's paying me. So I headed down to the library and checked the papers first. Turned out that Lady Nesbitt had rejected a generous offer from one of the industrial meat-packing operations in New Growl. One might have guessed they were going to take what they couldn't buy, but it didn't fit.

Corporations had time. Had patience. They wore you down with lawyers and accountants and paper cuts, and they always got what they wanted in the end. But murder? That's a more personal thing.

I dug a little deeper and found out that Deirdre's uncle owned a twenty-five percent share in Nesbitt's Fine Fish. Pretty worthless, when the company was barely scraping by. But that buyout would have had him living large for the rest of his life.

"It's a nice painting," I said. I wondered what it would be like to have all my ancestors staring down at me while I worked. "They all are."

Deirdre nodded and returned to her seat, her ears still twitching. "Thank you."

The plans I'd been thinking on the way up—a fire at the manor, a fall down the stairs—all seemed wrong. She was already standing at the edge of a cliff. All she needed was a nudge.

"May I give some unsolicited advice? Unofficially speaking," I said.

She pressed her paws against her cheeks. "I'm not selling."

"I've looked at the books. It's not good." I gestured towards the sprawl of red ink across the pages. "Besides, the stress isn't good for your health. If you sold, you'd have enough to retire. Even restore the manor, if you wanted."

"This isn't about me," she said. "This is about Beltham, and its future."

I thought about that run-down little village below the bluff. "Maybe they could use some fresh investment, too."

"Really, Mr. Stray?" She almost laughed. "Is that what you think Shrike-Pak will bring to Beltham?"

I stopped and thought about it. New Growl was full of factory castoffs.

Mangled legs, missing eyes—some of them would never work again. I walked past them every day. Sad faces with their hats upturned on the sidewalk, hoping for a handful of coins to get through the day.

Beltham had been different. Sure, it smelled a little funky, and the downtown had seen better days. But the people had been proud. Gull and ternfolk working side by side with droopy-eared bassets. Somehow, Nesbitt's cannery had built a community. Given its people a little dignity.

Still, I was here for a job.

"It's dangerous work," I said. "Better to be away from it. I mean, your father—"

"Yes. I know. The accident." She shook her head, and her fur gleamed pearlescent in the light. "He was a good man, you know. Working the overnight shift himself, so one of the packers could be home to see his litter born. Father always valued family above everything else."

"If he'd really valued family, he would have put you first, instead of the cannery. Then he'd still be here now."

"You didn't know him, Mr. Stray." Her eyes flickered shut, and her breath stopped for a moment. "It's hard to think about. I'll never forget that sound. All those hundreds of tins rattling around inside the coffin as they lowered it into the ground. I don't like to imagine him that way."

A shiver ran through the scruff of my neck. The newspapers had left out that little detail. I wondered how long Kenneth had been working this angle. I wondered how far he'd already gone.

"I'm sorry."

She looked up at me, fur bristling. "You understand then. This is how I keep him alive. By protecting this place. By doing the work."

"My lady, please," Mrs. Reed interjected. "You must stay calm."

Deirdre uttered a little chirp of frustration. "I'm sorry. It's just, this is very important to me."

"Perhaps a walk along the bluff? I can see to Mr. Stray while he finishes with the books." Her voice carried a glimmering edge of menace, but maybe that was just in her nature as a fox.

She nodded. "Yes. A walk would be good."

"I'd like to join you, if I may," I said.

Deirdre was already agitated. If I pushed a little harder, she might just cave. And if she didn't, a seizure along the bluff might lead to an untimely tumble. It was cruel, but only nature taking its inevitable course. And maybe more gentle than whatever Kenneth would arrange if I failed today—for both me and her. I'd already spent half the money in that envelope. There was no going back.

She eyed me, then nodded. "Maybe seeing what my great-grandfather built will help you understand what I'm trying to protect."

"No business talk, though," Mrs. Reed cautioned. She bit back a growl.

"Of course, Mrs. Reed." Deidre rose. "I'll show you the grounds."

Afternoon had fallen into evening outside, with the manor dressed in gold and bronze, and Beltham nestled in the shadows of the hills that embraced it. Streetlights flickered on, painting the buildings in an incandescent glow. The sky blazed a brilliant blue, and the ocean sang static like an untuned radio.

I followed the ghost across the sprawling patio and down a little foot trail beyond the gardens. This was where I'd first seen her, pale and drifting along the edge of the bluff. Already halfway to the next world.

I didn't like violence. I'd started out as a private investigator, trying to use what skills I had. But the work was slim, and there wasn't a lot of money in the cheating spouse game. So I took a few rougher jobs, until one day I crossed a line I hadn't known was there. But the war made a lot of us numb to things we wouldn't have imagined beforehand.

That's the world we live in. The rich could afford the veneer of civility, but the rest of us had to fight to survive. Whatever it took.

Deirdre seemed not to notice the precipitous drop that lay to her right, pausing only to point out landmarks in the sheltered cove below. The docks, the cannery, the fishing vessels. A church older than the village itself—a remnant of those that had lived in the valley thousands of years ago.

By the time the path ended, the village had fallen out of sight behind us, and we walked with just the churning waters of the bay far below us. Occasionally a distant wave caught the orange of the sun, flashing like a baleful eye in the deeps. The taste of salt hung in the air.

Deirdre came to a halt. I stopped beside her, a footstep away from the abyss. Close enough to push her if I had to. I didn't want to, but my shoulders tensed anyway. "It's peaceful."

"Yes. I used to come here with my mother," Deidre said. "Back when I was a child."

She still seemed half a child to me. I shifted my weight, wishing there were a better way. "You could let all this trouble go. Have a family. Bring a child of your own here, to share this view."

Deirdre laughed, a tiny, sad sound that caught in her throat. "No, Mr. Stray. If that really is your name." She twirled away from the precipice, and I heard the distinctive snap of a bolt-action rifle behind me. "I'm sorry to disappoint your employer, but I think I'll stay here and do the work I set out to do."

I froze. "What do you mean?"

"I mean that you've got one chance to tell me what Kenneth sent you here to do."

I turned slowly, keeping my arms by my sides. The ocean howled its mocking roar behind me. "I'm just an accountant, ma'am."

Mrs. Reed rolled her head, then flashed her needle teeth in a feral grin. "I called Barklays yesterday," she said. "They never sent that letter. There is no audit." She held the rifle with an easy grace, as if she'd been using it for years.

"It must be a mistake," I said.

"No, Mr. Stray." Deidre had her own handgun, a single-shot derringer she must have kept hidden in her dress. It was pointed at my chest. "You coming here was the mistake. So if you have anything to say, now's the time to say it."

"Please," I said, stalling for time to think. "Lady Nesbitt. I don't know how this misunderstanding came about, but killing me will only land you in jail."

She gestured beyond me. "The tide's coming in, Mr. Stray. By the time your body washes up, the crabs will have erased any evidence. Just a terrible accident."

"There'll be an investigation."

"And I'm sure my uncle will see that it's closed quickly. Wouldn't want anything unfortunate to turn up."

I was running out of straws to grasp at. I felt the weight of the revolver inside my coat pocket and weighed the odds. They were worse than I'd liked to consider.

Deirdre was a civilian. She might hesitate. And the fox's rifle was heavy and slow to bring to bear. If I threw myself to the side, I might get two shots off. Or I might be dead before I hit the ground.

"Okay." I told myself it was the math that convinced me. But I'd seen the factories in New Growl, and the truth was, maybe I was starting to buy into Deirdre's dream just a bit. "You take care of those people, Lady Nesbitt."

I left the gun in my pocket. I stepped backwards instead.

Sometimes staying alive means fighting against instinct. A cat always lands on their feet, but I tucked myself ball-tight instead.

Bounced against the cliff. Once. Then again. The world spun. My vision went dark, then flared electric when I hit the sand.

For a long moment, I was gone. Even more of a ghost than Lady Nesbitt up on the bluff. But it seemed I still had another life left in me. I dragged a rasping breath, reeking of seaweed, then climbed to my feet.

The gun was still there. Seemed dry, might even work. The rest of Kenneth Nesbitt's cash, too. I took a few pained steps down the beach, waves sloshing around my feet. Two ribs broken, maybe three, but that was the worst of it.

I had a choice to make, then. Climb up that hill and finish the job, or go crawling back to Kenneth and explain that I'd already spent his money. As if I didn't know where that road ended.

A crab scuttled across my path. I paused, wondering if there wasn't another way. I could let Lady Nesbitt report my death. They wouldn't look too hard for my body. Just another corpse at the edge of the Gunmetal Sea.

There were plenty of boats in Beltham. All I had to do was take one and see how far it would go. Disappear into that wild and roiling dark, and make a clean break of it in my last life.

And maybe, just maybe, things would come out better next time around.

THE PERFECT VICTIM

MEGAN LEE BEES

Forsythia Poppy Bunting might have been a rabbit, but she had newshound in her blood. She was a Class A wordslinger. She knew every which way to paint a picture in the rags, and she didn't need a thousand words to do it. So it seemed a particular unfairness that the lush, high-ceilinged, warmly wooded, richly carpeted abode she stood in could share the same designation as her thin-walled apartment down in the cannery district.

What a great injustice, that even when rich men fell, the depths they land in were far above her reach.

Poppy thumped her foot once against the thick Persian rug and wondered what a Cornish Rex was doing with such an artifact. If he was cousin to a Persian, or if this was some kind of cultural appropriation. Her nose twitched. Much as she adored her dear Deidre, Poppy never had much interest in the affairs of cats.

"Mind your foot, Poppy," she whispered to herself, and dipped a paw down into the bag she'd slung over her shoulder to touch the skull of her writing partner in thanks for the reminder. She didn't need her big feet tapping out her position and tipping off the downstairs neighbors while she prowled Kenneth Nesbitt's ostentatious apartment.

Kenneth was out for his dalliances at the local gentlemen's club. She had at least three hours to snoop before the cat came back. And for all the high class veneer of his apartment, it was considerably smaller than the countryside manor he'd grown up in.

That belonged to his niece, now.

Poppy visited Deidre as often as propriety would allow an old college friend.

Perhaps a few hours extra, but only because it took so long to bid farewell and close the door on Deidre's beautiful smile, her sad eyes and soft voice... It was likely that Poppy was more familiar now with Kenneth Nesbit's former home than he was, and the thought curled her lips in cruel delight.

His apartment was a mess. There were papers on the entry table. A hat hung on a lamp. Kenneth was clearly used to sprawling, and had exceeded the natural edge of his borders at least a decade ago.

"This is gonna be over in no time," she murmured to the skull, as she picked an unopened envelope off the top of the stack. Dues for his gentleman's club. *Final Notice* stamped in red across the name.

"Slovenly old git," the skull agreed in her own voice. "Bet he's got receipts for Deidre's assassin laid out on his desk."

"Now we just have to find it."

Poppy's nose twitched again, and she squeezed the skull in her bag to suppress the urge to hop. Ever since she found the skull in the back closet of a university bio class, forgotten, unlabeled, scrubbed clean of flesh, but the bone was stained with the memory of it, "finding" had become Poppy's superpower. Two heads were better than one, and the little shrew skull she carried in her bag was always with her, sniffing out the next clue though the nose had long rotted away.

Her talent should have made her famous. She was a marvel. She broke the story of Beryl Rambouillet's secret love affair before it was even a whisper through society. She knew what everyone was wearing, what everyone was talking about, months before the rest of the city.

She should have been working at The New Growler, with a

mahogany desk the size of a barge and twelve Puglitzer's to her name!

Instead, she was stuck in the tabloids, selling gossip to The Meowning Post. It paid the bills, sure, but Poppy was destined for more than secondhand suits and an ever-mounting tab at the bar below her apartment.

Thin walls, thin floors, rowdy drunks downstairs that kept her up all night. She complained once, just once, to the barback, and he said it was her problem for taking on the rent when she knew she had those overgrown ears.

Deidre loved her ears. She said she'd never met such a good listener. Such a good friend. Poppy could have listened to Deidre read the phonebook, if only to have a minute longer hearing that voice.

Something creaked in the apartment below. Poppy's ears pinned down to her skull, and the rest of her froze as her ears twitched and tracked soft footsteps that moved across the hall. Into the interior, kitchen. A cough. A running sink. Silence.

Her heartbeat slowed, and she tiptoed her way across Kenneth's apartment and pressed the door open to his kitchen.

"I'm really good at this," she whispered to her skull.

"Best in the business," the skull agreed.

The kitchen looked like Kenneth had stopped paying his maid a year ago and never bothered to ask her how to pick up a mop. Fish tins were left open on the counter next to stacks of dirty plates. Half-empty glasses were shoved all jumbled by the sink. Lamp soot and dust grimed over everything.

The white gloves she wore to disguise her fingerprints were already brown at the tips, and Poppy worried that her pristine white shirt would pick up dirt from the air itself.

"I don't think we can get through this place without leaving a trace."

The skull wheezed a laugh. "Guess we'll have to make a different one, then."

She smiled. "You always know how to cheer me up." Poppy enjoyed a good sneak, but it wasn't hard to throw anyone off her scent by turning an investigation into a burglary. She pulled open the liquor cabinet and was about to smash a bottle on the ground, when the skull shouted at her to stop.

"Get the evidence first!"

Poppy swooped the bottle up to take a hard swig of the brown liquid that burned all the way to the edge of her whiskers. "Shit! Sorry. Yeah, you're right. Two heads really are better than—"

"Focus, Poppy."

She nodded and set the bottle down. It was nice stuff. Maybe she'd keep the bottle and smash something else on her way out. Poppy allowed herself a quick perusal of Kenneth's liquor cabinet, but found very little worth smashing. All this grime, and Kenneth was still living the good life. She wore her very best suit to look like she belonged in this building, pressed her collar, brushed her fur until it shined, but it was still just single stitch, and underneath the dirt, everything Kenneth owned was gilded.

"Office should be up the staircase behind the stove. Press the cabinet in, and the false face will swing open."

"Right."

The skull was really her best asset. It staked out the apartment for a month while Poppy wrote her little gossip columns from the alley. It was the one who called the building's super, pretending to be an electrician to wire the old building for new lights, and got a floor plan for each. It set the time, it filched the keys, it hyped her up and promised to take care of her if anything went wrong.

And what could go wrong? It was already dead; it had seen the worst of the world and laid it all to rest. But with Poppy, it could do anything.

And it could easily pin Kenneth for hiring Deidre's ill-met assassin.

Deidre brushed the assassination attempt aside when she told Poppy, like it was a lark, a funny afternoon. She told her not to bother with it; the assassin was long gone, and her uncle wouldn't dare to try again. But that was the thing with Deidre. She was a kind soul, and she never thought she was worth the bother. But to Poppy, she was worth the whole damn world.

So the skull made its plans. It would break the story and give Poppy everything she'd need to be Deidre's hero. The skull may not retain any memories from life, but it seemed death had made it a romantic.

Poppy pushed through the cabinet and found the narrow servant's staircase that was probably made for mice. She pinned her ears down and crept up it, brushing her feet on each step to obscure her distinctive footprints.

"Leaving bigger marks that way," said the skull.

"You want us to use your feet instead?"

"Rude." It twitched imaginary whiskers. "Shrew feet are distinctive, too. If I still had them."

"Sorry."

Poppy couldn't take the full skeleton when she failed out of med school. She shouldn't have taken the skull either, but she couldn't just leave it there. Not after the late evenings they shared, the laughter, the joy. And when Professor Gosling couldn't even give her a name for Subject 308 as he dressed down all her shortcomings, telling her she was crazy, and that she'd never survive exams, she decided that he wasn't worthy of the shrew's continued tenure.

Deidre was the only one who still talked to her after she left in disgrace. Just Deidre, and the skull.

The office was an even bigger mess than the kitchen. It seemed to hold every scrap of paper that ever filtered through the mailbox, and all of it on top of the desk. Poppy indulged in a tiny, incandescent scream through her nose as an avalanche of paper sloughed around her feet. She hadn't even touched it! It fell at a glance!

"Calm yourself," coached the skull, and Poppy sat it down on Kenneth's chair. "What do you see?"

A fucking mess. She bared her teeth at it all, then breathed deep, and saw. Conspicuously empty trophy shelves. Paintings tipped against the wall. A safe, open, empty. If not for the stacks of papers, she'd have thought someone had already come through and ransacked the place.

Someone did; Kenneth. The floor was littered with receipts from pawn shops. Further down the stack, auction houses. He was selling everything he could to hold on to in this measly place, trading his name against the time he had left. Of course he was desperate to off his niece; she was the last thing he had left to sell.

The man held on to everything. All she needed was a name.

     THE PERFECT VICTIM

A slip of paper linking Kenneth to the crime. She could break the story. She could sell it to the New Growler. She could make her name and make good and ask Deidre to dinner—

But the light was fading. It filtered through the dusty drapery like weak tea, and Poppy looked over to the skull, who'd been trying to get her attention for an hour. "We're out of time."

A key clicked into a lock downstairs. Poppy's ears swiveled toward it, but she couldn't hear anything above the pounding of her heart.

"We need to go."

She palmed the skull and shoved it into her bag. She had nothing. Hours of searching through this festering pile of an old man's life, and he kept nothing that would implicate him in Deidre's assassination attempt. There wasn't a scrap of paper that even acknowledged his niece. Kenneth might have a dirty house, but he kept his paws clean.

Those paws stepped across the threshold and stopped. A low growl carried up the staircase. "Someone's here."

He had a stately voice, a higher timber than she would have expected, with that same elegant accent that drove Poppy twitterpated during late night study sessions at university. Poppy's skin crawled under her fur, to think that he could know Deidre so closely that they shared an accent, and to think of her as nothing more than an obstacle.

His paws moved further into the apartment, and Poppy leapt for the servant's staircase. She heard a lock click somewhere below as she thundered down the steps. There was a fire escape through the pantry, just across the kitchen. If he was going up, she'd go down. The skull cheered on her escape as she raced down, but as she opened the cabinet door, she was met with another click.

Keneth held a pistol, hammer cocked, aimed right at her heart.

"Big feet, little rabbit." His lips curled up at his terrible little joke and bared his teeth. "Why don't you sit down and tell me what you wanted here while I dial the police?" He stepped back and waved the gun toward a little chair in the corner.

He looked younger than she thought he would—or perhaps Deidre's gorgeously curled fur leant her a grace that made her seem older. His cold blue eyes were clear and piercing in the dark mask of his fur, his teeth polished and white as his jaw, his whiskers neatly groomed. The man took great care in his appearance and left his home to rot. How fitting.

Kenneth snarled and jabbed the gun at her. Her eyes flicked down to her bag. The skull shifted, gesturing to the chair. Better to survive the minute than test Kenneth's resolve. She dropped the bag and went to the chair with her paws raised high in surrender. She sat.

"If you're here for money, you're in the wrong place." Kenneth sneered down at her. "You'll find more loose change pick pocketing your average tom on the train."

She should have lied. The skull told her to lie, to play up the poor little rabbit who was just looking for a cashout. But she couldn't stare in this man's face and let him think for a second that she didn't know.

"I'm here for Deidre."

"My niece?" His eyes narrowed in confusion. "She doesn't live here."

She bared her teeth in a rage. "You tried to kill her, you son of a bitch."

"Ah," he said with a congenial smile. "I did no such thing."

He picked up the phone and dialed it with a single outstretched claw. His other paw kept the gun trained on her. A steady hand for an old cat; his vanity must have kept him in sporting shape.

"Hello, police?" He nodded at Poppy, as if apologizing for his rudeness; this would only take a minute. "It seems I've had a break-in. I've apprehended the culprit, but you'd better come quick. She looks like she's got quite a lot of fight in her, and I don't know what might happen if she goes for my gun."

He waited a moment, listening, then started at her, claw twitching on the trigger.

Poppy's heart jumped into her throat, and he gave a sharp cry and dropped the receiver on the ground. His pupils shrank to tiny slits, and he stalked close to press the gun against Poppy's racing heart.

"Tell me why I shouldn't shoot you now and let the cops clean up your body," he murmured in her ear.

A tinny voice cried out from the discarded receiver. "Sir? Sir! Sir, are you there?" There was no way the dispatcher could hear Kenneth's low growl over all the shouting.

Kenneth drew the gun away and fired it into the air. Poppy winced in agony, expecting to die, but the heat of the barrel was on her face, and her ears rang with the shot. Kenneth pulled the hammer back again and jabbed the gun into Poppy's ribs. The barrel scorched her white shirt. She could smell her own fur beginning to burn. The fire that fueled her righteous anger was snuffed by the cold glimpse of her own mortality.

"I'm a reporter," stammered Poppy.

Kenneth bared his teeth in disgust.

"I can make the truth whatever you want it to be. Swear to God." Her eyes darted around the room in desperation, but there was nothing to throw between herself and the gun lodged between her ribs.

"Now why would I want any more attention, when the little I have has got some desperate little sneak thief breaking into my apartment?" His eyes narrowed. "There was never a peep from my niece about any assassination attempt. Don't you think I'd have heard about that? Don't you think there would have been reports that one of the oldest names in New Growl was nearly killed?"

He stepped back and threw his arm across the counter, sweeping tins and plates and glasses onto the floor as he crossed back to the phone.

"No!" he cried, and gave a victorious smile. "Help!" He tore the cord from the wall and tossed it on the ground.

"You have one chance, rabbit. Tell me why you think I tried to kill my niece, and I'll decide if I need you alive to tie up any loose ends."

"Diedre," Poppy gasped. She didn't realize she'd been holding her breath until the name tore out of her like a sob.

"She's been talking." His whiskers twitched. "And she sent you here for proof?"

"I came on my own."

"Why?"

His eyebrows lifted as he asked. The answer was apparent on Poppy's face.

"You love her." He laughed. "Oh, you stupid girl. Did you imagine yourself my niece's rescuer? Saving her from her evil family? Did you know that she took that cannery from me? She has that place so subdivided between all those sad little families in Beltham that she's barely more than a figurehead."

He sighed and shook his head. His claw twitched on the trigger.

"Wait!"

He growled. "For what?"

"I can convince her to sign it over to you. She trusts me." Poppy's mind was spinning. She couldn't breathe, couldn't think. She had nothing but the next words out of her mouth to bargain against a few more seconds. "I promise. Look in my bag. I can prove it."

She nodded over to the bag she'd dropped on the servant's

     THE PERFECT VICTIM

steps. It held very little. Cab fare, a passport, and the stolen skull of a long dead shrew. "Don't worry," it said in a voice only she could hear. "I'll protect you, Poppy. I always will."

"What do we have in here?" Kenneth growled as he pulled it over to him. He opened it slowly, and the skull screeched "Boo!"

He dropped the gun, the bag, and his paling face looked up just in time to meet the bottom of Poppy's foot. She kicked him square across the jaw and scrambled to pick up the gun. It fired in her hands before she could even fully grasp it, and Kenneth slumped to the floor. Half his face was torn apart. One tall, proud ear was missing entirely, and stately fur was burned away and stuck to meaty flesh. He was still twitching, still gargling on the floor, and Poppy dropped the gun in shock.

"Run, Poppy!" said the skull. She snatched it up from the ground and shoved it into her bag, then ran for the fire escape.

Sirens were closing in. She had to leave. A window flew open as she thundered down the fire escape. A fox leered out at her, grasped for her foot, and she jumped on instinct, flinging herself far from the safety of the ladder.

Poppy fell. Her mind slowed.

"How many stories?" she asked the skull. It was in charge of plotting the apartment building. It knew every inch of the building.

Her arm hit the ground with a sickening crunch.

"Lady!" called the fox as he waved his arm from above. "Hey lady!"

"One," answered the skull. It's voice sounded funny. Garbled. Like it was talking around broken teeth. "You were on the last rung. Not too far now." She looked down at herself. Broken arm, singed shirt, face and coat covered in Kenneth's blood. "Keep going."

The fox was gone from the window, presumably to catch the cops as they surrounded the front of the building.

Poppy looked in the bag. "You're hurt." The skull was broken. Teeth knocked out, left eye disintegrated.

"Don't worry about me, Poppy. Get home. Go!"

Poppy spun on her feet and ran.

The story ended up on the front page of The New Growler, but it wasn't Poppy's name on the byline. She wasn't anywhere in it. A simple burglary turned deadly when the victim tried to apprehend the criminal on his own. Killer still at large.

Poppy set the paper down on her kitchen counter and rubbed at the cast on her aching arm. The vet said it was a clean break, but he looked at her funny when she asked if he could do anything for the skull in her bag. Threatened to call the mental ward on her, until she sweet-talked him into letting her go there herself.

She still had the number taped to her phone. She promised. She knew she needed help. That it wasn't right to keep somebody's skull in her bag, talk to it, make it her only friend.

But it wasn't her only friend.

She picked up the receiver, took a deep breath, and called Deidre.

   THE PERFECT VICTIM

MEI REN, ROYALTY

CAMDEN ROSE

By Camden Rose

"You're new here," the clerk said to me as he counted up my items: meal, grain, and a couple cans of Annelide worms.

I pushed my sunglasses up against my beak, hoping he wouldn't notice the blue ears behind my scarf. If he did, he might recognize me as royal, and I couldn't have that. Even if I was so far down the line of succession that I got all the work with none of the benefits.

"What makes you say that?" I asked, looking up, then down again. Nothing seemed suspicious.

"You're wearing sunglasses. Not even Bright Water has those mass produced yet."

"Oh," I said. I debated pulling the glasses off, but then my disguise would be revealed. So, I pushed them even further up on my beak until they pressed my feathers into my eyes.

I was stubborn, like Mother always said. Even though she'd done lessons with me for hours upon hours, trying to teach me the responsibility of Ren women to be strong, all she'd taught me was how to be stubborn.

"That'll be 15 pounds," the clerk said.

I handed him a 20 pound note. "A tip. If you'll answer a question of mine."

He shrugged.

"Have you seen this man anywhere?" I asked, pulling out a picture of my brother. It was a year old, taken on the edge of the east wing of our estate. It was blurry, but I didn't have time to get anything else.

"De Ren?"

Shit. He recognized De from the picture. That meant he

might recognize me as well. Then he'd turn me in to my family, and I'd be killed, just like Zhi.

Whenever I closed my eyes, I could see Zhi's green blood dripping out from between her scales. I wish I hadn't gone to check on her. I wish I'd been able to see more than the assassin's slitted eyes as they ran away. I wish I'd had a moment to give her a proper burial.

Instead, I'd leaned in close while she whispered, as soft as the sun, "New Growl. New Growl. New Growl." Then she pressed the photo into my chest.

And now I was here, in New Growl, already making myself known.

"But have you seen him?" I whispered, my beak clamped tightly together.

"No," he shrugged. "Sorry." He looked genuine. Not like Mother when she was apologizing to a commoner for raising taxes.

She'd always shared her true feelings with me after they'd left. Something about me being so far from the throne made me approachable to her, I guess. I wasn't a threat.

I handed him another few pounds, just to make sure he stayed quiet, and grabbed my food.

"Oh, and one more thing," he added before I could leave.

I turned, trying to hide my frustration. Mother said that was always one of my worst skills. I hadn't mastered hiding my emotions. I blamed it on the feathers that were always getting in my face, but she said it was just a skill I lacked and could never learn.

"Yes?" I asked.

He held up the pounds. "If you keep giving people money and asking them about De Ren, people will think you're from the crown."

I turned away so he couldn't see how right and wrong he

was. I was seventheenth in line for the throne. I'd never rule. And that's why I knew it would be a while before they came for me.

I had some time to find De. Even if I didn't have as much as I wanted.

"Thank you," I said, trying to sound grateful. Then, before he could give any more tips, I left.

The wind met me as soon as I stepped outside. It threatened to pull away the royal blue scarf tied carefully around my head. I couldn't have anyone recognize me this early.

New Growl wasn't in our jurisdiction, but our influence stopped only a few towns over. And the fact that the clerk knew who my brother was proved that I couldn't fully blend in here.

I needed to be smart about this.

Thankfully, there was traffic on this side of town, and I easily slipped through cars as I made my way across the street. It smelled horrendous, but no one else seemed to care.

I could hear De in my head, joking that the smell of fresh flowers followed wherever I went. Not anymore. Now I just smelled of wet and cold and gas and dirt.

Would I recognize De without his signature scent of burning incense? Without his nice suit? He would have had to change his wardrobe, his whole look, to survive. I had to hope he didn't have random clerks seeing through his disguise in less than a minute. Otherwise, he wouldn't have survived.

I had to believe he'd survived.

A tall stranger in the crowd shoved against me as I entered the stream of workers heading home. They smelled like daisies, fresh picked, and walked with perfect posture. I turned their way to yell at them, but they were already walking away, black coat flapping in the wind. Their hair was black, cut short, and their stature was straight and familiar. Not my brother, no, he had white hair like the rest of the family, but someone else. I closed my beak trying to remember why I knew them.

I tried running after them, but by the time I got out of the crowd, they were gone.

Maybe it was for the best. For all I knew, they were familiar because they'd assassinated Zhi and were now looking for me, too.

I tightened my scarf. I hadn't even been in New Growl for a full day, but the fear of the city was already sinking into me.

"Newspaper!" a boy no older than thirteen yelled from a block ahead of me. He held up a paper with the sign "VETERANS WELCOMED HOME" in big bold letters. Underneath was a photo of smiling men.

I crossed to the edge of the sidewalk. I didn't want a reminder that other people were happy. That other people gained brothers and spouses and friends around the same time I lost mine.

De had to be alive, so I could punch his shoulder and yell at him for leaving in the first place.

After a while of walking around New Growl with fewer pounds in my purse and fewer leads than expected, I finally accepted that I was getting nowhere. The sun was setting, and I needed a place to stay.

As I wondered down the identical corridors of the Mirror Maze district, I rubbed my feathers together to make myself as warm as possible. I should have figured out my living situation before investigating.

     MEI REN, ROYALTY

Did I really think it would only take a day to find my brother who had been missing for almost a full year?

Thankfully, as I passed by the ten thousandth boxy building, I noticed a sign leaning against one of the businesses.

ROOM AND BOARD - £15/NIGHT

That was a bit more expensive than most people could afford, but I only needed it for a few days. I knocked on the door, and an older lady answered. She wore large glasses on the end of her trunk, and through them peered at me as though I was a ghost.

"I'm here about the room," I said.

Without saying a word, she opened the door all the way and shuffled me through.

It wasn't much, just a bed with a meager breakfast of tree bark. I forced down what I could manage and went back to my bedroom.

Everything here tasted like it had been processed through ten different factories before it came to the consumers. And the store-bought stuff wasn't much better.

I swallowed my bile back down and opened a can of Annelide worms.

As I ate and tried to act like the bark inside my stomach wasn't attacking me from the inside, I tried to think about a plan. I needed to do something other than wandering around hoping to get somewhere. Something that didn't spend all my money in one week.

And that's when I reread the can's name. *Annelide worms. Made in New Growl.*

It was Mother who had first mentioned Annelide in passing, but at some point a couple years ago, whenever we talked about the proletariat, Mother stopped mentioning Annelide as being against us because of their consumerism.

She'd always been the kind of animal that hated anything capitalistic—it gave power to the businesses instead of the royalty—but somehow, at some point, Annelide no longer became part of the conversation. She just listed all the other factories instead: Nisbitt's, Greenry, and Shmultz.

I scooped out the remaining worms and dropped them in my beak.

Ze was the one who'd told me that Annelide was no longer part of the conversation. Then, he started disappearing for hours at a time and acting like he hadn't been anywhere. Whenever I asked him about it, he'd laugh it off. But I saw his eyes, the way they looked to the left like they did when he used to lie to our Mother about if we'd actually eaten all of our food.

And then, a few days after he lied to me again, he stopped coming back.

Mother told us it was a car accident, but I knew better.

His driver, Bo, didn't show any signs of remorse. If anything, he seemed like he was hiding something or was paid off to hide something. And a few weeks after De's disappearance, Bo quit.

My guess was that he'd made enough to retire and leave our crazy family. I'd do the same if I could.

It couldn't be a coincidence, the fact that Zhi sent me here, where Annelide had a factory. Something was up, and I needed to get inside to figure out what was going on.

And conveniently, I needed a job.

The factory was so big and tall that it blocked the cloud-covered sun. It loomed over me and everyone else in the area, just like the rotting smell, they were too used it to notice.

 MEI REN, ROYALTY

I stood there for who knows how long before finally heading inside. Workers left the factory with cuts, bruises, and missing limbs.

Once I entered, I wouldn't come back the same.

I took a step forward, the shadow of the building enclosing me. I needed this job, no matter the cost. It was the only lead I had, the only possible hint I had at my brother's disappearance.

I hoped I was right.

"I'm looking to work here," I said, stepping to the first animal who looked my way.

They gave a small eyebrow raise, as though they could hardly believe that I'd try to work there. They weren't wrong. Even today, though I'd abandoned my sunglasses and head scarf in favor of a hat, I looked out of place. The clerk from yesterday was right. I wasn't dirty enough.

"Through there," the worker said, pointing with their four-fingered hand toward a shadowed door.

I nodded and moved into the doorway.

The smell was overwhelming on entry. I knew Annelide didn't work with fish, but it smelled just as bad. Wrong, like a rotting tree. Fungal. Earthy, and off.

I stepped up to a man holding a clipboard.

"I'd like a job here," I said.

"Any affiliations?" he said, not looking up.

"No."

"Any previous injuries?"

"No."

He looked me up and down to confirm then went back to his clipboard.

"Any family members which might take you away from your duties?"

What kind of question was that? I hesitated. He looked up,

hawk-eyes meeting mine. I swallowed, looked down at the dirty floor.

"No."

He nodded, tucked his clipboard under his arm.

"When can you start?"

"Now."

He smiled, no teeth between his beak. "Perfect."

After he showed me my locker, he led me through the entrance to the main factory. The earthy rotting smell got stronger and almost made me faint. He threw a brown apron my way, and I barely caught it through my nausea.

I bet if De smelled me now, he wouldn't catch any fresh flowers.

"For the first hour, you'll learn the ropes from the shift supervisor, Amelia. Once you're good enough on your feet, you'll man the chopper alone." He motioned to a huge, rusty circle saw. It screeched as the animal behind it moved it down to chop the squirming worms on the conveyor belt in half. Guts spurted up at the worker, but they didn't seem to mind.

I gulped.

"Do I get glasses? Or goggles of some sorts?"

He laughed. "If you want to bring your own in, be my guest."

I nodded. For De, I could do it. I just needed to work here long enough to figure out if and how Annelide was connected to his disappearance.

Suddenly, a mousy woman appeared in front of us.

"Amelia," the guy said. "Meet your new worker."

She grunted and held out her hand. As I shook it, I tried not to think about how her hands were wet, and a deep cut ran across her thumb. It scraped against my smooth hands.

"Nice to meet ya…"

"Ray," I said. The word felt wrong in my mouth, but I didn't know who would recognize me by name.

"Ray," she said, whiskers twitching a bit. "Let me show you the chopper."

I nodded and let her lead me away, as I tried to not think about how many workers looked up at me from their stations with confusion and worry and hope and desperation, and maybe a bit of jealousy.

I wondered if I'd look like that soon.

It took me less than five minutes to learn I didn't like the chopper. If anything, I loathed it for what it was, how it smelled, and what it did. My left arm hurt, and my right arm throbbed, even though it had been resting.

Still, I kept working for an hour. Then two. At some point my arms went numb from pushing down the lever, even if I changed which arm I was using every few pushes. I was covered in worm guts and vowed I'd never eat animal again, even the delicacies.

I also started to realize why all the workers looked up when I entered. There wasn't much to entertain you here. All the stations were spaced out from each other, enough that we couldn't talk to each other. A few of the labelers in the corner were clumped together and talked on and off throughout the day, but everyone else was secluded off in their own corner.

Amelia checked on me a few times throughout the first hour, but at some point, she stopped coming. I only knew it had been two hours because the clock happened to be right across from me.

I knew this was part of learning where De was, but I was starting to wonder if I should have questioned workers outside of the factory first, instead of throwing myself into this. Or maybe I should have just let it be and not go after him. Maybe I should have just accepted that he was dead like Mother said.

It was in one of these intense bouts of doubt—I had lots of time to think after all—that I didn't press the lever down all the way. It slipped.

I fell forward, my beak crashing into the blade.

All I heard was the high-pitched ring as the blade came down on me. And then, nothing but blinding white pain.

I must have screamed, for the ringing stopped suddenly. Someone pulled me away. Amelia.

"You lasted longer than I did," she said with a careful smile. "The Chopper gets us all, eventually."

My face hurt, but I realized my field of vision was wider than normal.

"Nice haircut," someone from a station over yelled. Others laughed.

I stroked my forehead. All my beautiful white hair. Chopped down to barely a centimeter long. My hat was gone, eaten by the chopper.

I put my hands on my blue ears, now visible. Shit, shit, shit.

"We better get your beak checked out," she said, motioning to the place that throbbed.

I caught my broken reflection in the speckled and rusty chopper. My beautiful beak. It was dented pretty badly. I'd be lucky if it would heal on its own.

"Come on, Ray," Amelia said, pushing on my back. "Before the manager notices."

It took me a moment for me to realize she was talking to me. I grabbed my hat and let her push me away.

    MEI REN, ROYALTY

Amelia led me out of the factory to the heart of The Bellows. It was so bright. Was it always this bright? And this crowded? It felt like everyone was yelling, trying to push against me and Amelia, trying to stop us.

"New conditions!" some yelled.

"Protect our workers!" others said.

"Workers for justice!" workers chanted.

I closed my eyes, for a moment, to try to escape. Amelia led me through, and soon we were on the other side.

"Sorry about that," Amelia said. Her whiskers twitched as she grabbed her keys and unlocked a wooden storm shelter in front of us. "Normally, people don't get hired so suddenly, and I get a chance to warn new hires before they're put on the more dangerous equipment."

She led me to a bed-that-might-as-well-be-stone to sit down, then searched around for a light. When she turned on the lamp, I noticed my bed was actually a slab of hard wood with a sheet over it.

It was a small room, with only a bed, cabinet, and sink. The walls were dug out. She rummaged around the cabinet, pulling out a rotting apple, a bottle of clear liquid, and some towels, before pulling out a bandage. She came over to me and carefully wrapped my beak.

I froze, not sure how to process what was happening. After hours of thinking, it felt weird to talk, to engage in conversation again. Even if, as a royal, I was used to the poking and the probing.

In a few hours, I'd become someone different.

"Why?" I said, then cleared my dry throat. "Why are you helping me?"

Amelia smiled, pulled her ear. "You remind me of someone I used to know." She grabbed a cup and filled it by the sink. "Plus, you stick out like a sore thumb. If someone doesn't help you out, you're going to get chewed up and spit out by New Growl." She offered me some water.

I drank. It tasted disguising.

"How much are you making an hour?"

"I don't know. I didn't ask."

"Oh, Ray." She sat down next to me. "You should go home. This place isn't meant for you."

I shook my head. No. I wouldn't go home. Not when I was so close. Not when I had nowhere else to go.

"Getting splattered in worm guts beats being told what to do in the—" I stopped. I must be really out of it. I almost spilled my secret to this stranger just because she was nice to me. Had it really been that long since someone had been nice to me?

Yes, it had been. Even at the palace, I was alone. Zhi was my friend, but she was my servant. She was paid to be my friend. De had been a real friend, but he was my brother, and now he was gone.

They were both gone.

"Beats what?" Amelia prompted.

"Nothing." I needed to change the conversation. "Is this where you sleep?"

Amelia laughed, high-pitched and bright. "No. It's just a— let's call it an infirmary." She stood up, started putting every-thing back into the cabinet. "I have a place a few blocks from here. It's small, but it fits us."

"Us?"

Amelia paused for a moment. I debated retracting my question.

"Yeah," she said, closing the cabinet. "My family and I. Family is important to me. They're why I keep this crappy job." She stood up. "I should head back to the factory. You get some rest. I'll cover for you."

And then she left.

I tried to do exactly what she said, and I must have been exhausted because I slept like a rooster. Meaning that I had a nightmare about Zhi's blood covering my feathers. Green and sticky and hot.

It fucking sucked.

But what made it worse was waking up to a loud rattling.

I jumped up, reassured myself that the sound was not Zhi's dead body, and looked over at the culprit.

Halfway out of the cabinet, was someone with short black hair. They smelled of daisies.

Except this time I saw their face.

Bo. De's old driver.

"Mei Ren," he said, twisting his head all the way round to see me. "What are you doing here?"

"I could ask you the same thing," I said.

"I'm, uh, doing a maintenance check."

"Of the cabinet."

"Yes." He got up and brushed off his ruffled feathers. "This room runs the machinery for the factories down the street. I was just checking some pipes. You know, routine stuff."

"Checking some pipes in the cabinet." I leaned forward to see through the door before he could close it. There was some kind of tunnel, carefully covered by a collection of cabinet things. If I didn't know to look for it (and if Bo hadn't just knocked half the items off the shelf), I wouldn't see it. "Why is there a tunnel in there? And where's my brother?"

Bo's face dropped, and for the first time in the interaction, he appeared earnest. "Oh, Mei," he said, addressing me by my first name. That's how I knew he was serious. "De... he... he died."

I stood up. Bo was taller than me, but I tried to make myself look big by puffing out my feathers. All it did was accentuate the new haircut I had. I didn't care.

He was still lying to me. How much money did my family give him?

"No," I said. "No, he didn't. I know that he didn't. You lied. You were paid off. I just know it."

Bo nodded. He sat down on the bed, a cloud of dust puffing up as he did. "You're right. He didn't die then. He left. We left. Then he—"

He looked off in the distance, at the sink in this hovel.

"He'd learned about all the deals the family had made with the wrong side during the war and decided he was done with it. I didn't know this at the time, I was just his driver. But, when your mother paid me off to say that I'd killed him, I knew something was up."

Bo pulled at his coat. "I couldn't bear lying to your siblings' faces every time they asked. I couldn't bear lying to your face. So, I quit. And a few months after I left, I received a mysterious letter that I knew was from him. We met up, and he told me everything." Bo rubbed his ears. "We worked together to bring down the royal family. We collected documents and legal papers. And then," he looked at his shoes.

"He died," I whispered.

Bo nodded. "Somehow the family knew where we were. They knew that we'd be at Blue Grove meeting a contact." He sighed, looked at his dirt-covered hands. "There was a shooting. I tried to save him, but he'd lost too much blood."

I looked at my own hands. The same ones that were stained green not a few days ago.

"Zhi died, too," I said, though it came out barely audible.

Bo nodded. "She was our contact on the inside."

There was a long silence where none of us talked. I could

hear the traffic outside, the workers getting off, the wind rattling buildings.

Life moved on. De and Zhi were dead, but life moved on.

"I refuse to let their deaths be in vain." Bo stood up, turned toward me. "Help me, Mei Ren. Help me bring down Annelide and the rest of the royal family all in one swoop."

He pulled out some crumpled papers from under his coat. I read through them, quietly, slowly.

Annelide, during the war, had been funneling messages in their cans. Not just messages for our side, but for the spies, too. Whoever paid, whoever was willing to take the risk.

And when my family found out, they didn't ask Annelide to stop. Instead, they let Annelide pay them to be quiet.

And even though the war was over, Annelide was still paying.

"Do you see now? They're evil," Bo said when I looked up from the last document. He rolled them up and tucked them back in his coat.

"I—" The next words wouldn't come. I didn't know what to say, honestly. Mother always talked about how she didn't like capitalistic systems, that it made money the most powerful motivator instead of the royals, but she let herself be bought all the same.

I knew our family was fading away, but I didn't know that they were that desperate.

I'm sure they'd covered up many scandals before, but this was different. This was a scandal that showed whose side we were really on. It would turn our remaining allies against us.

"I need your help, Mei Ren," Bo said. "We have resources, we have people, we have plans, but we lost our Zhi. Someone that the royal family trusts. Who better than the young princess who ran away because she saw something she shouldn't have? The one who needed some space to breathe but was now back and ready to be part of it all again? We need you to help us. We already have the bomb built, we just need you to set it."

"A bomb," I repeated. "You have—but that would kill…"

"They've already killed many of ours. Including De and Zhi. All we're doing is stopping more from dying. Amelia clearly trusted you, because she brought you here. Show us that trust was true."

I stared at Bo, who didn't seem to realize what he was saying. He held out his hand, urged me to take it. Urged me to become a murderer, just like the assassin who killed Zhi.

I couldn't hurt what remained of my family. Not like that. I couldn't hurt *anyone* like that.

"I need to go," I said, my thoughts clearer than ever.

I needed to go back. I needed to warn them. I needed to tell them so they wouldn't get killed, too. I didn't like Mother, but that didn't mean she needed to die. She needed to know that there was a whole organization plotting against her.

"Ren," Bo said, "Please." He grabbed my hand. It was warm, trusting, and tight.

"Let me go," I ordered.

Bo let go, eyes wide. He knew what it meant to be ordered by royalty.

But still, he looked hurt.

Before I could change my mind, I pushed open the storm shutters and left.

The crowd met me as soon as I stepped outside. The bustling threatened to pull me away. Nothing had changed. The protesters still held up signs, chanting. The newsboy still yelled about the latest post-war efforts. The workers still hobbled to their injury-prone jobs.

And then there was me.

I started walking south.

Amelia was the one who brought me to the room. She must have seen my ears and made the connection.

Did she also want to kill the royal family? She complained about her job, sure, but she had a family to care for. Could she really find a safer job fast, especially once she was marked a killer?

I wished for my scarf, for something to keep my face hidden so I could sneak back into the crowds without feeling like they all knew who I was.

Everyone felt like a suspect. Everyone felt like someone who might be part of the assassination group Bo and Amelia were in. Beaks and eyes and heads and trunks all turned my way.

And then, I recognized one of them.

The assassin. The one that had killed Zhi. He was uncovered here, but the slit eyes were unmistakable. The cat-like reflexes.

I turned, but the crowd was thick as honey. And with my tears, I had a hard time finding a path out of the masses.

And then, he was on me. Gloved hand around my wrist. And I knew he wouldn't let go.

He pulled me through the crowd—why murder in a busy street?—and I tried to pull away, but it did nothing. I screamed, I yelled, I bit him with my throbbing beak, but nothing worked. No one seemed to care.

We left the crowd. And before I could say anything, there was a bag over my head. It smelled wrong—too clean.

"Nighty night," the assassin said.

I woke to jostling under me. My guess was that we were in a car.

"And the city. It's truly abysmal this time of year." A controlled laugh. "Though it's always abysmal."

Mother.

I tried not to move, but she must have noticed a shift because the conversation stopped.

"You didn't use enough," Mother said.

"I'm sorry, Chun Ren. I didn't want her to—"

"What? Die? She's already dead to me." Silence. "Well, take it off already."

And then, brightness. My guess was right. We were in a car. Outside the window, the congestion of New Growl was replaced by open fields and bright sun. We were heading back to Sinnal. The place where I grew up. My home. The palace.

Mother sat facing me, her hands clasped in front of her. Lace everywhere, just like always. On her gloved hands, within her dress, and on her hairpiece.

"My, you've really let yourself go," she said, with an eye flick toward my hair.

Mother was always good at showing the micro feelings. When I was a child, she used to get upset at me for not being subtle like her.

"Why don't you just kill me, too?" I spat.

I hated her. She'd killed De. She'd killed Zhi. She'd allowed Annelide to kill others in the war.

"Too?" Her left eyebrow went up, just a bit. Then she relaxed and closed her eyes to show she was in power. She knew I'd do nothing. She leaned back in the chair, but still kept her perfect posture. "Oh, Mei. You really understand nothing."

I kept quiet. It felt like a trap.

Mother leaned forward again. I could see her eyes through her perfectly curled white hair.

"The only people that matter in this family are the women. The royal women. We're the ones that others notice." She leaned back again and looked out the window. Her beak caught a shadow, and as the car moved, the shadow twisted and curved like a knife. "You may be far from the throne, but you have a reputation to uphold. If a servant or a man goes missing, no one cares. But a Ren woman?" She flicked her wrist, barely. "We can't cause a scandal now, can we?"

My beak hurt, though this time from clenching it tight. Part of me, the part that was as frustrated and angered by this as Bo was, wished I'd said yes to the bomb. I could blow Mother up right now and end it all.

But even if Mother died, someone would ascend to the throne. There was always someone who wanted power.

"But now you're back," Mother said. "And now you've learned about the responsibility you bear. To the throne. To me."

I wanted to snap back at her, to tell her that all I'd learned is that everyone is an asshole, including her, and that I'd have no say in this. I wanted to jump out of the car, run back to New Growl, and convince Bo and Amelia to not kill my family, or they would be killed too. I wanted to bring my brother back, bring Zhi back. I wanted to bring back everyone that my Mother or the royals before her had ever killed.

But something Mother had said stuck in me.

The responsibility you bear.

She was right, but not exactly. I had a responsibility, but not to the throne, and certainly not to her.

I had responsibility to the people like Amelia and Bo and the clerk.

Maybe I wouldn't ever be the queen, maybe I wouldn't even get close enough to be a formal princess, but I could gain Mother's trust, so she let me in on her secrets. So she let me help her make decisions.

But to do that, I needed to act like someone I was not. I needed to act like a loving daughter.

Acting had never been my strong suit. Amelia and the clerk were testaments to it.

But, I didn't need to act like I was from New Growl. I just needed to act royal. I just needed to get close enough to Mother that she wouldn't even realize I was whispering revolutionary ideas in her ear. She already considered me not a threat. I just needed her to trust me as well.

Even if it took years.

"Yes, Mother," I said, bowing low so she couldn't see my rage.

TAURIC TONIC

PEN ANDERSON

By Pen Anderson

I've a story that starts out at a club in Soho, 1933 about me and a lady I had a thing with. It was pretty dark how things ended. Maybe, now that I think about it, was dark how things started as well. I could have been the bull in her china shop of emotions, rather than the white knight I had hoped to be.

She always looked like she was enjoying herself. That pup could make anyone feel like they belonged right where they were, talking to her. Lynette's homey, best friend glow even extended to the serpentine gentleman across the bar, though it didn't quite shine on him the same as everyone else. He stood, a Northern slow worm dressed in tweed and tartan. The loose grip he had on his cane belied the aristocratic airs I got off him. His small eyes locked on Lynette, unblinking, like he owned her.

And on that evening, he might have gotten a little closer to it. We were celebrating. It was a few hours into the night, and the lame Scottish lizard had recently bought a stake in our little dance club on the edge of Soho. Nate Challtainn had signed up as a silent partner. He wasn't going to run things, but he promised to keep us afloat whenever we'd need it, with entitlements.

Lynette was pouring all of her special kinds of social lubrication, keeping the club's cups from ever running low. She'd been behind Dexter's bar all of the last three years. But, me and that slab of wood were all that was keeping the reaching patrons from grabbing her soft, bronze curls.

They beg for her to come out and wait tables, let the hounds sling the bottles. She'd huff at the suggestions and laugh at the paws reaching out, but if anyone ever got within even an inch of her long, lustrous ears, I'd make sure that inch was quickly expanded to feet or miles.

Coming up behind Lynette to put his arm around her was my man, King-of-the-Jungle Dexter, the "Dex Callaway" in "Dex Callaway's Catbaret". His ginger mane waved through the air around his head, haloing him and Lynette both. Dex flushed with rose under his blonde fur. He raised his voice to chat up Challtainn and called for another round.

Dexter waved me over. They'd put back a few nips before he detached himself from Lynette.

"Ian! Nate wanted your opinion on something."

I walked over. Lynette was already reaching for the kettle before I said anything.

"I heard you won't drink, mate," Challtainn said. "But you ought to be celebrating with us. What'll it be then?"

"She knows what I like," I said.

"Oi loik!" Challtainn mocked my accent, grinning. "You fit a sharp suit though, my boy. Something out of Savile Row."

I nodded. At my size, I couldn't fade into the background even if I wanted to, with a white pelt that shines like the moon and black marking my snout and sharp points. I fill doorways. My horns snag chandeliers. I rock boats and carriages. I turn heads. I can't ever claim to be invisible, so I might as well be worth looking at.

Dexter leaned forward, excited about something. "Nate was just telling me about Berlin. The clubs there, Ian. They seem to be really together. Knowing what's right for each other. They feel like family more than business."

"Everyone doing their part," Challtainn agreed. "That's the key. No one trying to hold on to more than their share."

I didn't say anything. I'd heard Dexter go on about Germany before. How they'd been getting the country back on its feet after the War and the Depression. Though I didn't care what went on over the Channel anymore, we had been struggling here. If it gave Dex the drive to work hard over here, couldn't be a problem, could it?

"Alright then, I know we're celebrating me coming on and all, but I can't stop this nagging me." Challtainn set his glass down, looked at it for a while before looking back at me. "You do good here, for sure. You're a face, and a body, that people know around here. But—" He licked the air. "I'm only just getting to know you now. You're not in the game for business, are you? You just want to work? How much would it take to buy you out?"

Lynette fumbled the kettle, and a splash of hot water soaked the counter. Dexter grabbed a towel behind her, but didn't seem to hear Challtainn.

"I thought you lot already worked out your share," I said.

Challtainn's head turned back to the bar for a moment before continuing with me. "My apologies. You're absolutely right, my boy. Here, I've come in with my grand offer, and you already nabbed it. The goods already sold. Who am I to ask or offer any more?" He barely paused for a reply. "Think about it, though. You could still work, earn a salary. Everyone benefits. Everyone knows their place. Nobody loses."

"Just me and what's mine?" I asked.

He shook his head. "You'll still be family, like Dex was saying. Everyone has their own part to play. I can do more for you with your share—I just wasn't sure of that until I met you."

Lynette set my drink on the bar. Hot tea with a splash of lemonade and a splash of grenadine. Over the ruby-tinted drink, Lynette's eyes locked onto mine to let me know she had thoughts, but wasn't going to say anything now.

I took my tea, kept my eyes on Challtainn as I lowered my head to drink. The points of my horns dipped into my vision. I told him, "I'll think about it."

After close, I went straight to my flat and got a solid three hours before waking in a heavy sweat. Dreams and headaches kept my sleep light, and damp. I washed off with the sun shining into the windows. Lynette showed up at my flat, knocking as I was getting out of the bath. I answered with my towel around my waist. Water dripped off my shoulders onto the floorboards.

For a moment neither of us said anything. She was looking up at me. Her dark brown Cocker Spaniel snout pointed up from my bare, pale chest's height, but she kept eye contact. Her eyebrows shifted slightly over her seeking, amber eyes. We'd been there before, stuck trying to read each other's minds.

"Come on," I said, before the shadows lengthened any more. "I'll get dressed. You know where everything is." I left the door open for her and headed back to my room.

"Love, I'm sorry," she called after me. "I'm just banging on your door when you're trying to relax."

"You're all right!"

When I came back out in shorts and a vest, she was at the kitchen window, looking out into the garden. I had washed and dried off, but seeing her coat catch the shine of that golden hour light made me start to sweat all over again.

"I think he was serious about that offer," she said without turning around.

I ignored that. "Now that I'm dressed, can you give a bloke a hug?"

She turned. Smiled, but there was an effort to it. She embraced me, warm and solid against my chest. Her head tucked into my shoulder. It was uncomplicated.

We let go before it became complicated. She quipped with a mock and a cock of her brow, "If you can call that dressed, you actual layabout!"

"Yeah, I'm a cad, you can say it." I thumped my chest, and we had a good laugh.

Her gaze drifted back out the window to the garden as her laugh weakened. "Do you remember when you used to talk about retiring in Suffolk?"

"Where my parents are from. Where my parents' parents were from. I don't know that I ever stopped talking about it. You're just—"

"Not around as much, yeah. You said that before, too."

"How much more are you going to read my own biography to me, pup?"

"Don't call me that." Her ears shook. A squeak snuck into her voice. "Blood, Ian. Three years you've been calling me that. Three years ago I told you to stop. I've been waiting for—" She stopped, shook her head. "Do you ever want anything besides a nice suit?"

Her anger caught me off-guard. "I don't—"

"No," she barked. "Listen to me for once." Her eyes were shining, pink around the edges. "You're going to refuse that buyout. I know you are. You're going to make some noble stand about what's right, about not being pushed around, about principles. And Challtainn is going to destroy you for it."

"It's our club."

"Is it?" She took a step closer. "'Our club'? You worked yourself half to death. Worked almost every forsaken night to keep Dex's running smoothly. You've covered for girls coming in late or missing shifts, handed out money you'll never see again. You hooked up folks with more than booze and don't talk to anyone about it. You make sure everyone *else* is taken care of. Always. And you're getting twenty percent? You're thinking that's what you're worth there?" She panted. "And, now you haven't said nothing, but I know what you're thinking."

"Yeah, I think you said it right there, what I'm thinking."

"It's not about that. It's about what you're worth, but it's not about what your cut is worth." She left her mouth open to say more.

I waited for her.

"Alright. You remember the bloke from Peckham, or Charing Cross, was it?"

I did as soon as she said it. "Peckham."

"Back in the early days. I think I had only just started working, right? It really set a tone. You could set a tone then, too."

I didn't respond to that.

"We called for the doctor. And when the sergeant came, we told them it was an accident, that he was drunk, that he fell." She sniffled. "And—I've watched you carry out hundreds of drunks. You're always so careful. You've never hurt anyone who didn't need maybe a little bit of hurting, just to calm them down. You're efficient—you gotta be when dealing with those louts— but you're not cruel. I know it doesn't take much for a big beast like you to take another, smaller beast down."

"I appreciate your review, but you're being vague."

"Challtainn has photos from that night," Lynette said. "Dex never told me where he got them, but he told me what they show." She looked away again, delaying what was weighing her down. "That you had him in a headlock. That it looks like you snapped his neck."

"That was years ago. How could they say something now?"

She took my hand in two of hers. "He told me while opening the club last night. Casually, over slicing limes. He was talking about the deal with the Scot. He told me your cuts, and when I confronted him about how you were getting fleeced, I guess he felt pressured." Still holding my hand, she said, "He told me about Challtainn's photos, what he knows. But he also said he talked Challtainn out of blackmail." She sighed and dropped my hand. "But... I guess that went some other way. I can't tell with him anymore, with Dexter."

"Yeah, some other way. So, what? If I don't take his offer then?"

"I don't know, but I don't like it."

"What's there to like?"

"He made me an offer, too."

I let her go on.

"My own club at a hotel. Full management, forty percent stake. Dex Callaway's Brighton." Her voice was hollow. Her shoulders sagged. "Dexter said I deserved it. That I'd earned it. And I am so excited. I love the seaside. But he kept talking, and I started worrying. He started talking about you again. That everyone would benefit if we just cooperated as a 'good family'. That he expects you to 'play your role'."

I didn't know what worried her, so I told her what I did know. "You have earned it."

"It can't be like this." Her brassy brows furrowed as she dug into mine with her sharp, amber eyes—their pink edges still had my attention. "Ian, listen to me. I don't know what Challtainn is capable of, but I can suspect. He's rich. He could buy us without flinching. He could buy anything. Why does a Scot do business in Germany? You have to take the money and go."

"Go? Why?"

"I don't trust Dexter anymore, either. He's been talking about the Scotsworm like he's Dex's lost mentor—or father." Lynette shivered. "It could be that Dexter thinks he's helping you. I want to think he really does. But he's starting to sound like a newsreel from Berlin. He talks to me sometimes, after he's given you one of his philosophy talks. He thinks there's a proper order to the universe and a proper way to get things done, and you're 'just a bloke who won't step up'." She put on a mock of his growling cadence when quoting him. "But the Germans will, and Challtainn is his gateway to Berlin."

I was reminded of something Lynette had said to me after our thing. She looked at me while I lost focus for a moment.

"What won't I step up to?" I asked without looking at anything.

She touched my face, bringing hers back into focus. "You think wanting something makes you selfish. That's why you think fighting for Dex's club is noble. You say it's yours, but you're willing to take less than a third of a three-man operation. You might even make some noble stand about being able to prove yourself to the law."

"And where would that put you? You also gave your statement to the sergeant." I snapped my jaw shut. I realized that I had walked into a trap.

"Take the money, Ian. Be selfish for no good reason. Go to the fields and farms you told me about. For once in your entire life, just run away and be happy. Because, even if you're right. Especially if you're right…" She put her other hand on my face, pulled my snout down to hers. Quick and fierce, a nuzzle and a kiss, and suddenly she stepped back. "I still can't save you if you won't save yourself."

She left me in the kitchen. I was letting her go. Again.

I stood there thinking that she was right. That I was going to refuse the buyout on principle. That I could survive anything they threw at me, and she would be fine because all would go right. I didn't realize that she was right about everything else she said as well.

They came around to my flat that evening, before opening. I was out in the garden when I heard voices from inside.

Dexter's voice carried through the interior. "Ian, mate, we need to talk." His sonorous purr had a cheerful benevolence, like no matter what he was about to do, it was a favor and a blessing.

I went in to meet him. Dexter was standing in my front room like he belonged there. Challtainn was by the door, between us and the exit. Both of his hands were on his cane, but he didn't say anything.

I stood in the space between my rooms. "What's this about?" I asked.

"Just a conversation," Dexter said.

"This feels awkward, friend."

"I apologize, Ian. I just can't be at the club tonight, and I wanted to pitch in on the offer before we go."

He was hitting me on two sides at once, and I wasn't sure which new fact to respond to first.

Last in, first out, "I gave my answer."

"No," Challtainn spoke up. "You didn't."

Refocusing on Dexter after Challtainn, I saw the folder in his hands. The edges of its contents made pale creases and cracks in its waxy finish. Dexter held it out to me. The red bow of its clasp reminded me of a Christmas gift, and something in his grin gave me the uneasy sense that he might be happy to give me this misfortune.

"You remember our night talking to the bobbies a few years back?" Dexter's voice was gentle, like he was explaining something to a child. "I know, not a month goes by that we don't have some cleanup to do. Drunks fall, get into scuffs. You carry them out, call an ambulance, make your report. But this was the big one. The absolute tragedy."

The folder had the photos Lynette had warned me about. They were a bit grainy. They had been blown up and cropped from a photo of some other subject. I'm sure it was taken from outside Dex's. The jazzy spectacle of fashion often drew society hawks and newspaper hounds. Everyone wanted to show off their tassels and plumage as the night sky descended onto the street with the sparkling stars of flashbulbs. It could have been any night. Grainy, mostly black, but there I was, a glowing white blur with stocky horns just barely in focus. But, I knew it was me, cradling the bloke from Peckham in my arms. It was the kind of image which could suggest anything. For proof, the only matter was who was doing the talking. And who was doing the listening.

"I heard that the family never got any closure," Challtainn said. "Very sad. Of course, if they saw these photos, they might want to reopen things. Police could want to revisit any statements they took." He looked towards Dexter. "I think I could vouch for the lion. I have clout, you see." He looked at me. "I don't know you. I don't know the girls. How many witnesses said they saw anything? Do you know?"

"Listen." Dexter didn't let me answer. "I'm trying to help you. We both are. You're being selfish right now, and I know that's not who you are. You're better than this. I wish I had time to explain everything I need from you, but the freedom to make investments is something we always agreed I had. That you didn't want! You've carried so much. Now's the time to lay it down. Make your sacrifice, my oxen brother. We need your blood more than we need you."

"My blood? You've always had my blood. My sweat. Lynette brings in customers, but I make them feel safe."

"You think that's what they're there for? To feel safe?" Dexter guffawed. "No, these lambs get their comfort at church, not the cabaret, poor sop. They're there to feel excited, get in trouble. You bring them danger, not safety. You're a giant. A challenge." He laughed some before going on. "I am genuinely surprised— no. Well— Yes, I am surprised that I did not expect you to really think that way about my club—"

"It's our club," I blurted.

"Oh, ours, is it?" Dexter composed himself. "Yes, ours it is, or has been. You've done the work. We've run it together. We all put in the work. But now you want to hold on to more than your fair share. You're a perfect specimen of your kind, but I don't need a bull or an ox now. What I need is more dogs." He grinned, and all I could see were his finger-length canines. "I know you know how to put the dogs first."

I looked at him. The lion whom I served with as brother-at-arms against the Kaiser was now siding with his inheritors. He says they're a new breed of German, but what does that mean? That war was a lifetime ago, but everything I hear from them is a reaction to it. I barely even remember the me I was back then, living automatically. The past three years? Running the club had made something new out of both of us. I started to wonder then who was doing the most running. I wondered if I had been mounted like some American rodeo bull. I thought we had been a team, hauling down the road together. But, has he been riding me this whole time?

"No," I said.

Dexter shook his mane. "What?"

"No. I'm not selling."

"Wait there, Ian. We've talked about things like this before, remember what I told you about the origin of all the species, and our roles in this world? Challtainn gets it, the Germans get it. I know it's beyond you, but you have to understand that I do understand it."

"I don't need to make this sacrifice. These photos are extreme, Dex. Can't you see that? I hear about your loving Germans kidnapping all sorts and deporting them without any trials. They only want, what, rabbits and cats and dogs running shops? No one with horns?" It didn't feel real to me that anyone could classify thinking, feeling beings like that. "We're not machines, built for a single task."

Silence. Then Challtainn laughed—a wet, gargling chortle.

"Well," he said. "That's disappointing. Callaway, my boy, I don't believe he'll be golfing with us any time soon."

Dexter's lips curled to reveal the peeking tips of his ivory canines. The skin over his nose wrinkled. "You're blinding yourself, Ian."

"Good. Then I can't see whatever shite you're trying to push at me." The photos were out of the envelope, resting on the table. "I can't see how these could be meant to convince me, either." It looked like a game now, and I meant to call it. "I think you're bluffing."

When I looked up from the photographs, Dexter was staring at Challtainn, who was holding out a pistol. The small revolver was targeting my wide chest.

I jumped towards Dexter without thinking. I heard the gun go off, but he missed somehow. My hand caught Dexter by the throat, and I lifted him off his feet. He clawed at my arm, but it didn't loosen my grip. I kept spinning.

As Challtainn aimed the pistol for another shot, I threw the lion at him. Fur and linen crashed into scale and tweed as another shot threatened to deafen the three of us in my narrow apartment. Dexter crumpled over the reptile, dragging him down.

Challtainn did not wait to scramble up from underneath. He used his cane to pry himself out. Callaway slumped to the floor, and Challtainn reached for the gun he'd dropped. I didn't let him get that far. My fist slammed into his gut with the full strength of a beast of burden, and he folded over it. I grabbed him by the collar before he could drop and held his licking, scaly face to my heaving, black-skinned snout.

Challtainn coughed before a grin spread on his cracked,

scaly lips. "Oh, I always looked at your fur, but aye. I should have known your flesh was dark."

"Ian, what are ya doing, mate?" Dexter was getting to his feet, sliding up with a lean against the door. An arm held limp.

Challtainn spat at me. "You can't be reasoned with, cow."

He raised his cane and dropped the head of it onto mine faster than I could react. I felt something snap just under the base of my horn, and my forehead felt warm.

As my vision blurred, Challtainn slipped out of my grip.

Dexter let out a pained roar from his place against the door. "Nate! You can't!"

My reason responded fast enough to the clues, and I reached back to grab the reptile from where he was able to retrieve his gun. One hand grabbed his cane arm, while I swatted away the gun with my other hand. He didn't get a chance to level it before losing it again.

My head pounded, but I had both his wrists in my hands when I pounded my head right back at him. I swung left, and I felt my right horn contact scales, tear flesh. I swung right, and I felt my left horn snag his wobbly neck. It wasn't as flexible as it looked, and I heard a covered snap like I had never heard before.

His head slipped off my horn, and his body fell.

The flat went quiet except for Dexter's breathing and my own heartbeat pounding under my horns and, what felt like, through them.

"Jesus, Ian." Dexter's voice was shaking. "What have you done?"

I couldn't see him, and I couldn't answer him.

"Ian."

I spoke up through the overwhelming headache. "Get out, Dex. Leave the photos. I'll take your deal, but you need to give me everything you can tonight to buy me out."

"I can't. I needed his..." Dexter stared at Challtainn's corpse coiled on the floor.

"Bollocks!" My mind was looking for exits and blockades, anything to prepare for whatever was next. "Just get out." I pointed at his dead arm. "Stay out of the hospital for a day, if you can. I think I'll need some time."

I don't know how long I stood still in my flat after Dexter left. Some blood from my forehead had run down into my eye and dried there, gumming the lid half-shut. Electrical jolts ran up the core of my horn along with my pulse. But since my stillness didn't stop the pain, I got moving. The flat carried a vague, foreign smell I recognized from the trenches. Gunsmoke. Comes to mind anytime I consider travel. I haven't left England in a while.

When a knock came, I thought it was a memory of the morning. It was so familiar and so distant. In and out of my concussive daze, I almost didn't answer.

Lynette let herself past me as soon as I opened the door. She dragged me into the kitchen for the light, which still wasn't good enough for her. She thought my eye was a wound at first, but brought her hand to her face after she got me sitting down next to the kitchen table.

"Oh, Ian. Oh, stupid love."

"What are you doing here?"

"Dexter came to me." Her voice wavered with a concealed worry. "His arm's broken, he thinks. I didn't see any blood, but he wanted me to see about you." She stopped, shook her head.

"He was crying, Ian. I've never heard him cry. He kept saying he didn't know Nate would pull a gun. That he never wanted this."

"He brought this."

"I know." She found a towel to wet at the sink. "Sit down. Let me look at your head."

I sat. She stood over me. Cleaned my eye, dabbed at the wound. Her fingers were gentle around the base of my horn, probing the edges of whatever had cracked there. She pushed in the middle, and I jerked. In spite of the attack, her scent took my mind off the smell of violence. A cool breeze dragged around her ringlets.

"It's not as bad as it looks," she said. "Squish but no crunch, not broken. But you'll have a scar. And you probably have a concussion."

"I'm starting a collection."

She didn't laugh. She kept cleaning, working the dried blood out of my eyebrow, my eyelid. Her face was close to mine. Despite her coolness, there was a ragged anxiety to her breathing. "Dexter said you agreed to take the buyout."

"I did. After."

"After you killed, um, him." She looked around.

"After he tried to kill me. You're cleaning up his first attempt now." I followed her look. "It's gone now. I took care of it."

Her hands stilled on my face. "It?"

"You were right before. I don't know Dexter. You say he sent you here? But why? What's he going to do now?"

"I didn't want to be right. But don't worry about him. What are you going to do now? You're leaving?"

She set the reddened towel aside. Her fingers lingered on my jaw. In the middling light of my kitchen, she looked at me for a long while. I would have thought I'd want to kiss her then, but something made me feel like she was further away than I was.

"I don't know that I can afford to."

"Even with the buyout? How?"

"There's no buyout without Challtainn. Dexter made that obvious before I kicked him out." My horn pulsed with electricity again, and I closed my eyes. "I don't want to see him again anyway."

Lynette waited for me to open my eyes again before saying, "I have some saved. Not much, but enough I could surely get you to Suffolk. I can have it for you in an hour."

"Please, no." I was already thinking of another way.

"Don't." She told me. "Don't you dare. You said I was right about everything, didn't you? What about what I said about your stupid nobility? I can help you." She pressed her snout to my head, careful of the wound. Her lips rested on a dry part of my pelt. "You stubborn, bullish ass." She pulled back and wiped her eyes. "I can help you, and you can help yourself. Don't keep fucking up, Ian."

I pulled her close. I pressed my nose into her neck. She started shaking. We both did.

She broke the silence with pragmatism. "I don't know what you did with his body, but I'm sure you don't have forever before someone comes looking for him."

"I'm sure I don't."

"You need a story that holds, Ian. Dead investor, you gone— that still looks bad. But where the hell is he? I don't even know what to say to cover for you now."

"You don't need to cover for me. I've got something I can do. You go on with your life. I'll see you at the club on your next shift, but that will be the last time."

"It doesn't have to be. I won't be there forever."

"Brighton?"

"Eventually. Who knows? Maybe I'll go to school in France, follow my family line back like you are with yours."

"Lynette. I'm not—"

She held up her hand. "If you say my name like that again, I won't be able to do this. And I have to do this. Because you still don't know how to save yourself, and someone has to."

She went to my bedroom, came back with my old army bag, started packing for me, emptying out small portions of my drawers until she filled it.

I watched her while my head swam, and my mind raced through everything I ever said and never said to her. But now, it's just too late. I could have, for any other circumstance but this. But I can't stay here, and I can't be near her when all of this comes down.

I took the bag from her after she finished. I'm not sure why, but I was holding it as I walked her to the door. I probably should have kissed her then.

I made the train to Southampton with minutes to spare. Bought a last-minute coach room ticket with cash I grabbed from a spot in the club's office the night before. I got a glance of Lynette working at the bar as I tried to sneak through. Her talent enveloped the patrons as ever. I lingered to watch her work, but she never looked my way.

The next sunrise I watched from the deck of a ship—England and Wales already lost to the horizon.

I stood at the rail for a long time. The wound on my head had scabbed over, ugly and still throbbing. Wind tickled my horns. I'm sure I looked smaller. I felt shrunken, lost. I knew where I'd end up, but I didn't know where to go from there. I wondered what I wanted, and I kept looking back to the sunrise.

ONE KILLER DEAL

PHOENIX BOURGEOIS

By Phoenix Bourgeois

It wasn't as hopping as the Wild Hare, or as howling as The Alpha on a Friday night, but Vix liked the ambiance at the Fox Den. The red-tinted lights. The beaded chandeliers. The shadows. The vintage brass ashtrays with hairless motifs. The jazz was steady, and the bartender knew how to make a proper martini—gin, and dry, with a caterpillar twist. If she was to meet this detective, *Det. Angelica Dam*, according to the fax sent to her agency, Vix would do it on her territory.

Detective Angelica Dam entered the Fox Den at precisely six o'clock. Leporine, wearing a velour fedora, ears perked out the sides—unmistakable as a sore thumb at a poker match. *Or a rabbit in a fox den*, Vix thought.

The detective ordered something with hops at the bar, snowball tail twitching through sensible, off the cob grey trousers. She wore scuffed wingtip oxfords—flat. No polish. No color. Not even a lifted heel. *Why do all detectives insist on dressing in black and white?* Vix observed discretely through thick, coal lashes, taking another sip of her martini with pursed lips.

Vix had done a little sleuthing of her own. Research, if you will. Preparation, as with any business meeting. And to Vix, it was *all* business. Detective Angelica Dam was a transplant to New Growl. From somewhere up North. Cold. Dry. Somewhere without as much mud. She'd hopped after a bad marriage. A broken career. Gone private to make a new name.

Dam looked the part, gray rain slick trench coat and an all-too-serious demeanor, but young. *Jumpy.* Vix supposed she shouldn't call the *burrow* black. She herself had risen in real estate at a dizzying speed. She'd earned her success, teeth and claws. Business was roaring. Done were the days of dusting off brownstones in the dregs of Willows Weep, wetting her fur in Bog Town, or carrying an umbrella when it *didn't* rain at the Crows Nest.

Vixen Underwood had *made it* in this hoof of a city. Sure, she had scars, but couture and concealer hid most of them. Champagne and growlers of giggle water hid the rest. Vix absently toyed with the long strand of white pearls at her neckline. Diamonds flashed on her ears, almost as white as her canines. She'd dug her way out from the Eye, where property was stolen more than it was sold. Before, she couldn't rub two coins together. Now? Now, she paid for her Pawda in cash. Vix twisted an auburn curl behind her ear. She was living her dream career, and she would be damned if anyone threatened it. Especially someone wearing *velour*.

"Vixen Underwood?"

Detective Angelica Dam made her way across the smoke-laced lounge. Shorter up close. Square backed. *A doll and a detective.* Attractive dame, in a dowdy, depressing way. In a way that made you work for a grin. Vix sniffed the air. Detergent. Petrichor. A faint aroma of wood smoke and straw-bed. Dry sweat. Vix narrowed her amber-yellow eyes and smiled, more sharp than welcoming.

"It's Vix. Got a flame?"

"Quit." Dam flipped her chair around and sat, legs straddling the splat back. Toes scraping the floor. She cracked her neck. Set a rain dappled wax cotton briefcase on the table between them with a soft thud. Vix pursed her lips and snapped her cigarette case closed.

"Pity," she pouted. "How can I help you?"

Jazz musicians shuffled past them to arrange their ensemble of instruments onto a cramped corner stage, wedged in with gilded patina mirrors and sparkling pendant lights to make the space appear larger. Vix enjoyed the intimacy.

"Tell me what you know about Hopper," said Dam, taking a careful sip of her beer. Lips pursed, asymmetrical. A lick of foam clung to her whisker.

Vix frowned. Suppressed a shiver. The metallic, questioning buzz of a cornet sang out beneath the warming lips of a bovine player. The seating lights dimmed, but the hush of the crowd vanished as swiftly as it had formed.

"Trent Hopper? No beating the gums, huh?" asked Vix.

She didn't like where this conversation was going. Detectives weren't good for business—as a rule of claw—but Vix dealt with her fair share of feed. Decent ones, dirty ones. *Decent dirty ones.* Most often, they wanted information on clients. The lowdown. The dope. The flap. Locations of love nests or dens of vice. The occasional private access to an occupied listing, the chance to check the drawers.

She'd play ball, if she didn't have to give up the whole game.

Vix hadn't spoken to Trent Hopper in a shave past six months. *Professionally*, of course. He was a wealthy broadcasting tycoon. Business type, mercurial. Handsome—for a vegetarian. She'd sold him a penthouse at The Crescent in Bright Water. High Stable Street. *Under* asking. In this market! Good client. Better commission. Vix told Angelica Dam as much, signaling the bartender for a second round. Oh, how she loved to talk nest.

"Trent Hopper was found poisoned in his penthouse."

That stopped her short. The rest was unspoken.

In the penthouse you sold him.

This time, Vix let the shiver of cold shock run its course, raising the fine tuft of fur on her neck. This was no interview, it was an interrogation.

"Is he okay? Did Trent—Is he—alive?"

The detective's silence was answer enough. Trent Hopper was dead.

Vix blinked. *Trent Hopper, bumped off. Thank the hairless gods the check cleared!* She'd sold deathplaces before, but usually the body was cleared out before it sold.

"Where were you, the last night of the last full moon?" Dam asked.

Vix scoffed. "I'm a *carnivore*, darling. Not a killer."

A waiter deposited Vix's martini. A serpentine fellow, whose service Dam waved off. Dam continued her questioning as he wound back into ambiance.

"How is this not front page of the New Growler?"

"Company wants it quiet. Did you know Trent Hopper submitted a permit to remodel The Crescent the week before he died?" Dam asked. "The blueprints show most of the dwellings in the building demolished. Bye, bye, condos. Hello recording studios, business suites. An exclusive music club on the entire lower level. A restaurant, the works. *Hopper Towers.*"

Vix shrugged. "Mr. Hopper is a broadcasting tycoon. He has the lettuce. Sounds swell." She pawed her hair past her shoulder and fiddled with her watch.

"*Was* a tycoon. Before he was found dead in—"

"Yes, yes. The penthouse I sold him." Vix rolled her kohl, fox-lined eyes.

"You didn't answer the questions."

"No, but that is what you are getting at, right? I sold Trent the penthouse he died in, and now I am a suspect? Why isn't the police handling this?"

"Oh, the killer's caught," Dam said. There—the barest hint of a smile. "The police caught him holding the bag. I was hired *before* Hopper's death. To investigate a different crime."

The band started in earnest now.

"Oh? What crime would that be?" Vix asked. She feigned indifference with a swish of her tail, but a cold sweat, not unlike the perspiring rim of her freshly shaken martini, formed on her body. Vix snatched at her glass—the garnish was making a run.

"You didn't just sell Trent Hopper the penthouse. You sold *the entire building*."

Ice snaked down Vix's spine. The shadow of a smile settled on Dam's countenance, ill-fitting as her trench coat. The real estate agents at Habitat 20 were as bubbly as freshly popped champagne, but Vix sold it sharp. Like this detective—neat. She respected it, despite the sour feeling brewing in her gut.

"What are you talking about?" Vix's brow arched. It was a question in the way raised hackles were an invitation. *An invitation to scram.*

Vix popped the wriggling caterpillar between her fingers into her mouth and gnashed with a satisfying *squelch.*

Dam pointed to the briefcase. Opened it. Drops of water danced in dappled cast shadows as Dam pulled out an envelope in a sickly yellow hue. Tapped it. Slid it across the table with a curved, un-manicured nail.

Vix drained the last mouthful of vermouth-soaked gin. It burned more than it ought to. The smudge of red lipstick on her martini glass looked dirty, and Vix resisted the urge to wipe it clean. Voices floated in from the pool hall, buoyant, too loud. The hideous mustard-yellow parcel was heavy in her hands.

A mournful saxophone lamented, backed by the trill of rising percussion.

Vix ignored the gummed flap and slipped a red-lacquered nail straight into the crack of the corner and sliced down with a slow and serrated rip. She let the documents fall to her lap.

The first item was a glossy brochure from Habitat 20. Ink-drenched in luxury real estate, her smiling face front and center. *Only the finest in New Growl.* Below the brochure was a thin stack of black and white photographs. Her sharp lacquered nails made crescents in the photo paper.

"Hop off it, pal," Vix warned.

"Don't call me 'pal', *foxy.*" Dam's voice was incessantly calm.

The detective took another painstaking sip from her beer, appraising Vix. *More foam.* Vix's lip twitched, but she forced it down before it could become a snarl.

A dossier! A dagnabbit dossier.

"Drop the veil, Jumps," Vix said. "Cut it straight and we'll have time for another cocktail." Vix ran her tongue over her canines. She dug in her designer pouch for matches.

"Perhaps you should switch to coffee."

Vix went deadly still. She eyed Dam as one might dinner.

"I like my coffee bitter, like I prefer my dates," Vix growled. She couldn't help but ruffle her fur. It was a defense mechanism. "Thanks for being so accommodating."

If this wasn't terribly inconvenient, Dam would be her type.

"Part of the job, sugar. I'm paid to follow the tail," said Dam. The corner of her mouth curled upward, but veered into a straight line. *Almost missed the light.*

Vix flicked a spent match, trying to remain calm. In real estate, there were no 'good bones' without the flesh. Vix ate it whole and spat it out polished, ready for the dotted line. She didn't promise potential. *She sold dreams.* Everyone had them, even Detective Angelica Dam. Vix eyed her tip to tail in study.

"We're alike, you and I," she said.

"What, both agents?" Dam asked without humor.

"Both lonely."

For the first time, Dam looked caught off guard. Like she caught a mouse instead of a carrot. Her nose twitched. *And how!*

There it was. The trap was set. It was worth the pang of

emptiness in Vix's chest. The voicing aloud of the hollow feeling that kept Vix hungry for *more*.

Now it just needed springing.

"You wrote to me *four days* ago." The grit of Vix's voice was as low and slow as the sap from a sugar maple tree. "Why wait until Friday night? Unless you had no one else to go home to? The case is hot. Hopper's body is cold. And your divorce—and everyone you know—is a train away from New Growl."

There was a heartbeat of silence after the dying drums of the last song.

"*That* is none of your business," Dam growled.

Her voice was as cold as glass. Quick to shatter.

"I *make* it my business to get to know all of my prospective clients," Vix said. The blood on her hands was as red as her lipstick, and Dam knew it. Vix shifted. She tapped her heel on the linoleum. She leaned in for the kill. "Everyone in New Growl has baggage. That's what the extra bedroom is for." Vix edged forward conspiratorially, with a feline smile. "I hear you had a bad rap in your last career, Angi—can I call you that? Forced out."

"Police work is tough, Angi, but detective work is tougher. Especially in New Growl. *Much less support.* Irregular paycheck. It would be a shame if you stepped in the wrong puddle here, too. But don't worry. I can show you how to stay dry."

The jazz jogged to a higher tempo, the horns grating.

Vix leaned back and spread her arms wide. "Finding shelter is what I do."

Now Angelica Dam was livid. Vix tossed her lush red curls and straightened her shoulders, fanning herself with the brochure.

I do love playing with my food.

Dam gulped the last of her beer and slammed the mug down. Foam-stauche city. She balled her hands into fists. "Here's what I think. I think you are as crooked as the sign on this bar. Every tenant was forced out of that building, and each ploy smells more and more like you marking your territory." Dam pointed an accusatory finger. "Trent Hopper needed that building. He had you do his dirty work, and I'm guessing for a pretty tip."

"You convinced folks it was time to sell—time to buy—time to scram. You spread stories about pests and health hazards. Faulty wires. You linked up other agents. You paved the way for Hopper Towers better than the bulldozers."

Vix's heart beat in her ears. The lounge flared red.

"A tall tale. But mine's longer. And you have no proof."

"Every tenant I spoke to received your business card and brochures."

The music crawled under Vix's skin. She crossed her arms. "So has half the City. No crime in good marketing."

"*Hmph.*"

Trent Hopper was dead. *He* signed the contract for Hopper Towers. Her role had been minuscule. Almost imperceptible. A drop of blood in the sea. Vix had just been doing her job. Folks migrated all the time. Different roosts, and all that.

Besides, the rules in New Growl were different, if you knew which game you were playing. Clearly, this Detective Angelica Dam did not.

"Get off my tail," Vix warned with a low growl.

The jazz ensemble broke into a cacophony of discordant tones.

"This was no gat or chipper," Dam pressed, raising her voice above the din. "Trent Hopper was poisoned with *your stories*. Lead. Arsenic. *Mold.* You're lucky it's not you on the floor."

The joint sharped to a single edge that fit in the space between Dam's lips. The space where '*your stories*' was uttered.

The words that would cling to Vix's soul even as she vehemently denied them.

Vix shoved her chair backward.

"Time is money, and this isn't worth mine." With hands shaking for a smoke, Vix retrieved something slender and gold laced from her pocketbook. "Here's my card for next time you're in the market—housing, or otherwise."

As Vix stood to leave, the detective's hand leaped out to encircle her wrist. Her chair scraped to a halt. The cold metal of Vix's engraved gold watch and the flicker of seconds pulsed between them.

Dam's gaze was hard and steady. Green eyes. Sparkling. Twin headlights about to run her over.

She jerked her head to the table. "You forgot to tip."

"Here's a tip for you—" Vix leaned in close enough to smell Dam's musk. She let her composure slip, venom seeping into her tone even as the jazz rang sweet. "—live in New Growl long enough, you'll become the villain too."

"Is that a confession?"

"It's a warning. Call it a *lesson*." Vix paused, indignation and vermouth warm in her chest. "Or an *invitation*, if you still feel lonely."

Dam's grip twitched. Released. Her shoulders slumped, then straightened.

"Right. Bye, doll." Vix winked on the way out.

On the stoop, Vix opened a black umbrella, careful not to wet her curls or the sleek highlight of rust-red fur at her ears. Prone to frizz. Heart racing. She strolled with confident, even, clacking strides. Her heels weren't made for running, unless it came with a paycheck.

Agent Vixen Underwood paused in a cone of streetlight across the misty street, curious if the detective would follow. The air was cool on her flushed cheeks. Vix lit a cigarette with her last match, one ear perked for the imaginary sound of sirens. With the waning moon overhead, she watched the partially obscured silhouette of Detective Angelica Dam as she put her fedora back on. The waiter appeared with another drink. Vix took a deep pull, and the ember burned as bright as her amber eyes.

Your move, Dam.

WOLVES ALWAYS HOWL TWICE

H.L. FULLERTON

By H.L. F ULLERTON

From inside Halya's Teas & Leaves, Mohair Eaves watched a bruiser of a rhino wearing a quartz-studded monocle and an equally sparkly, astrological-themed cape wriggle free from the driver's side of a new meringue coupe he'd just illegally—and crookedly—parked beside a fire hydrant.

Halya's was a tea shop that sold tea and fortunes, coffee when pressed. The flashy mammalia Perissodactyla—of the unicorn variety—uncorking himself from his latest frippery was the shop's namesake and resident tasseographer: Halya. It was the fortunes Halya told in the back room of his shop that funded his divine fripperies. The tea was brewed and served by a round-robin of zebras, one of whom was shaking their mane at the boss' latest overindulgence.

Mohair was at their usual corner table, their back to the door. But that couldn't stop them from enjoying Halya's entrance. People tended to forget that a rabbit's widely spaced eyes were as good as a rearview mirror, better actually. Mohair liked to practice using their $360°$ sight, solving crossword puzzles, and listening in on other people's conversations. Partly because rabbit ears were top-notch for overhearing secrets, but mostly because jobs weren't as easy to come by as New Growl's press officer would have you believe. Especially the type Mohair was interested in. They had caught a taste for spying during the Sokol Salad Riots and continued spying well after anyone was willing to pay them for it.

But being a rabbit in the private inquiry field wasn't easy. Appearances were everything, and Mohair's narrow frame and curly mop atop the typical lagomorph visage didn't shout *I will eat your enemies for breakfast.*

With most of the citizenry of New Growl believing that sharp teeth made sharp minds, most of Mohair's cases were subcontracted from larger firms who were willing to hire an investigative rabbit situationally (when underestimated and overlooked was needed), but not permanently because, well, appearance, appearance, appearance.

Their stock-in-trade was affordable inquiries for the average Joe, which didn't lend itself to affording office space. Mohair longed to resolve the type of intriguing situations glamorous people stumbled into. It was Mohair's keen observational skills that noted Halya wasn't wearing his usual wide-brimmed hat as he passed by.

"Where's your hat? You lose it? Want me to locate it?"

The rhino patted his bare head. "You jest. Funny rabbit, car is my new hat. Mr. Sun cannot burn me through my metal friend."

"A coupe isn't a hat. It's more like a jumpsuit. With a hood."

"I'm not wearing no crook's jumpsuit. I earn an honest living."

Which sort of depended on how you felt about astrology and fortunetelling. Mohair knew what side their greens were picked from, so let that slide. Halya let them use the back room to meet clients when he wasn't meeting his own. Gratis, ever since Mohair had sorted a vanishing stock situation.

"Well, your coupe isn't striped. It's more like a fancy wedding cake. Do I hear bells in—"

The ding of the shop's bell announced the arrival of a paying customer, and the banter stalled. While Halya might predict futures, Mohair Eaves could sense when an animal needed help, and when an otherwise glowing middle-aged mare in a fashionable chartreuse and cream silk skirt suit confidently walked into the tea shop, they immediately spotted the hitch hidden in the golden horse's stride.

She was a beauty in trouble.

Mohair's nose twitched at the delicious combination of rich wife—noting the pair of Gradl's rings (the go-to jeweler's wedding collection from two summers ago) upon her left hand —and thorny secrets. The great unacknowledged equalizer in New Growl society was that even beautiful people had ugly problems. And ennuied spouses were Halya's scones and jam clients.

So when the mare approached Mohair's table after ordering an iced chai with oat milk instead of discretely slipping into the back room for a tea leaf reading, and said, "Are you Mx. Eaves?", Mohair mentally accepted the case sound unheard.

Hearing her trouble only strengthened their resolve. Mrs. Nougatte-Nury explained how she was being harassed by a wolf who'd already wrecked her first marriage and was now attempting to ruin her second. He was sending increasingly threatening text messages. She quoted a few from memory as she handed a sheaf of papers to Mohair who quickly glanced at the first page with its declarations of adoration, its *tell me you feel the same way*s, its increasingly demented demands to meet, then tucked the rest away to go over later.

"Do you recall the Breezer Bites scandal?"

"Which sport's that?"

That got a head toss. "Football. My Mackie was a star. Tin attacked my dear Mackie. So vicious. Everyone said. He never played again: Tin. Mackie would've. The Growlers offered him a contract. It's why we moved here, and then—then he killed himself. It was all so terrible, and now it's happening all over again! I think Tin might hurt me this time. Or worse, go after Meret." Meret was her second husband, the buyer of the Gradl's rings and—presumably—the square cut emerald and enamel pendant playing peek-a-boo with her unbuttoned placket. "When you read all the nasty, vile things Tin says..."

Mohair sympathized. A wolf having you in their sights was never a pleasant feeling. "Have you gone to the police?"

She snorted. "They won't *do* anything. They think it's wolves being wolfish. Probably think I've encouraged him. What's the old saying, 'They can't chase you, if you don't run'? The police can't understand. But you do, don't you, Mx. Eaves?"

Mohair did. "Mrs. Nougatte-Nury—"

"Call me Bibi. After you heard such private things, it feels like we're instant friends. I could really use a friend."

She dabbed at her eyes with a pocket silk, lightly smudging her makeup, which revealed the weariness and age it'd expertly masked.

"I'll see what I can do," Mohair promised. They'd save Mrs. Nougatte-Nury, *Bibi*, from the wolf knocking on her door.

"Thank you. Meret thinks it's nonsense. But he doesn't know Tinny like I do. I'll feel ever so much better knowing someone capable is involved. That someone can stop it."

They forgot to ask who referred her, but a rabbit with a nose for dirt and eyes on the big time didn't closely examine a gilded horse's mouth. They did, however, do their research and dig down deep into the past.

The wolf nipping at Bibi's heels had a short career in football and currently worked in the corporate accounts division of The ASH Group, specializing in customizable corporate retreats. He travelled frequently and was never in the office or available by phone. Mohair suspected Tin Silbursun-Howell did as little work as possible. No one at the company was forthcoming with information about him or their retreats, which wasn't surprising since The ASH Group was owned by Silbursun-Howells.

There was definitely something fishy going on at The ASH

Group. On paper, they looked legit. They operated resorts and hotels all over. Frequent injections of capital seemed to come from family members with careers in professional sports. According to news feeds, they recently acquired the Night, Owls! chain known for catering to both diurnal and nocturnal guests with convenient check-in and check-out times and separate wings for day and night sleepers. Yet, the family's meteoric success from one struggling lodge in Lake Forster to hotel magnates (with their flagship lodge and resort now nick-named Lake Four-stars by the bee-havers) struck Mohair as suspect. Possibly less than legal. Which might go far in explaining Tin Silbursun-Howell's short-lived career and even shorter temper.

Yet Bibi may have exaggerated her first husband's stardom. He received a lot of press for being one of the few turtles in foot-ball and did several advertisements for roadsters and revitalizing supplements. Mackinaw and Bibi Nougatte appeared in the gossip columns like clockwork; pics of them in their glad rags graced many a society feed. One clipping had a wolf in the back-ground who could've been Tin Silbursun-Howell.

Mohair also located the vicious *Breezer Bites!* vid of Silbur-sun-Howell and Nougatte brawling on the pitch. Rehashing the fight dominated the sports feeds for a week or so after, and both players were officially reprimanded by the league. A month later, Mackinaw Nougatte's suicide revitalized the whole brouhaha and then... nothing.

Tin Silbursun-Howell vanished.

There was a property owned by the wolf in West Chirrup, but the home's occupants were a Gold and Carat Char-Ash, a lupulella and a chrysocyon (ages unknown). They were regu-larly joined by a dapper wolf (name unknown, but who Mohair suspected to be Tin Silbursun-Howell). What was the story there? Renters? Lovers? Accomplices? Mohair really wanted to go to West Chirrup and surveil the property, but that was more curiosity than anything to do with the Bibi's case.

Mohair wondered if The ASH Group might have any corporate dealings with Meret Nury. Nury was a horse with his fingers in a lot of pies, including a construction company that consistently won bids on city contracts and being part of the consortium that owned the New Growl Growlers—the same team Bibi said offered her first husband a contract before his death. Mohair wondered how involved Meret had been in offering that contract or if he'd even known about it. Records showed Meret and Bibi married eight months after Mackinaw's death.

Mohair visited Meret Nury's office and requested an appointment, but the administrative assistant there insisted there was no time in Mr. Nury's schedule. He was a very busy horse, what with the Growlers' stadium renovations underway. She helpfully confirmed that the team did use a hotel chain under The ASH Group umbrella for away matches. Mohair succeeded in getting Meret on the phone once, long enough for the stallion to interrupt their introduction spiel with, "Don't waste our time. Bibi's 'prowler concerns' are all bugs and bull." Then dial tone.

Further calls went unanswered. No matter. When Tin Silbursun-Howell resurfaced in New Growl, Mohair had a plan to deal with a wolf who wouldn't take *no* as an answer.

Then Meret Nury disappeared, and Bibi was worried the wolf would come for her next. "It's Tin, I know it. He's behind this. He took my husband! What do I do? Is my Meret dead? I can't bear it. Oh, Mohair, you have to do something. You have to stop him!"

Mohair felt out foxed, but promised their client that a determined rabbit could out badger any carnivoran. They'd dine on their client's enemy's bones—metaphorically. A new plan was hatched on the fly.

Tin Silbursun-Howell knew all about being watched. For a time, he'd been watched professionally, then professionally hounded right out of that career—so yeah, he was familiar with how it felt to have someone follow his every movement, and he was practiced enough to parse the difference between an appreciative audience and a not-so-appreciative one. He also prided himself on being able to sense the weight of recognition in an animal's gaze, and while the eyes he felt upon him as he cha-cha-cha'd and mamboed his way across the well-enough-maintained but equally hard-used parquet floor at Dance-Dance didn't fall into the category of I-know-you-and-remember-what-you-did, they definitely bordered on I-know-your-type-and-you-don't-belong-here. And strictly speaking, Tin didn't belong at the redundantly named dance hall. He wasn't a regular. Had no intention of becoming one. Had picked it out of a dozen possible spots because of its downscale ballroom vibe, which meant it was unlikely to cater to the crowd where anyone would know him. Sad fact was a well-dressed wolf would always be suspect to some.

Let them suspect. Tin never held much with the nature-nurture harpies who screeched about the carnivore-herbivore distinction. Hadn't before he'd been vilified on sports feeds worldwide because of his "true nature" and certainly didn't now. Unfortunately, someone here at Dance-Dance seemed to subscribe to a wolf-eat-dog (and everyone else, too) worldview. While twirling his assorted dance partners across the floor, Tin spotted the watcher: a wallflower rabbit lurking near shadows and corners, looking like a judgy fog about to charge up a mountain it clearly held in contempt. The rabbit didn't chitchat or dance—any comers were rebuffed, such that all others veered clear. Tin had to consider the likelihood the rabbit was working up the courage to either confront him about something or ask him to dance—and time was running out.

The night was winding down, the band neatly transitioning from the blood-thrumming notes of the Tortuga Tango into a waltz which Tin recognized, but couldn't name. He was better with people than things.

The lovely kudu in a purple drop-waist fringe he expertly guided into a splashy spin to end their dance was Lalah. She had the hint of a beard that she'd dyed an almost match for her facial pelage and the smoothed stubs of removed horns he glimpsed because of the exaggerated head flinging she engaged in during their tango. The thrashing had drawn attention he could've done without, but almost everyone's gaze flew to Lalah, glanced off him, then returned to the attention-magnet kudu.

Had anyone an inkling as to his infamy, Lalah's spectacle would've clinched it. There were enough years between him and the debacle that the panic he felt was a tiny drip of a thing that could just as easily been caused by the fear that Lalah would slip from his fingers and thunk onto the maple parquet—an embarrassment for anyone who prided themselves on their dance prowess and might even be showing off a bit in hopes that the wallflower rabbit—the one with severely cropped bangs and curling tuft-topped ears standing at attention, the one in an unflattering suit, the one who stared all evening, would toss caution to the wind, approach him for a dance, and feel welcome and included in the evening's fun. Neither happened.

Tin danced his final waltz of the night with Alex, a Kodiak who talked the entire time, repeatedly calling him "Tim" and insisting "Tim" had played third base for the Stingers, right? Wrong. That was *Tensley* Hoel—still not a Tim. A distant cousin, to be sure, but an entirely different animal playing an entirely different sport. (Who Tin *may* have impersonated once or twice, when it suited him, but tonight wasn't one of those times.)

"It's Tin," Tin finally said, his ears going flat. "With an 'N'. As in: Nice waltz, but I've got to go." And not just because of the misnomer.

On the last one-two-three of their box step, Tin caught sight of a woman who could only be there for him and was so out of place in Dance-Dance that any caption in tomorrow's rags would include the phrase 'slumming it.'

Alex waved him off happily as the bear had already caught sight of the glittery sophisticate and beelined toward her. Not about to be caught in the same trap a second time, Tin used the bear as a screen, slinking out of the hall via the staff entrance before anyone could photograph the lady and him in the same room and flog it to every gossip columnist in New Growl salivating at the change to slap a slanderous headline over scandalous innuendo and call it a scoop.

Tin went back to his hotel and reminded the front desk not to confirm his presence or put through any calls. Since the Night, Owls! chain was a subsidiary of the company that employed him and was run by his mother, he felt confident his privacy would be maintained. In his room, he changed from his three-piece gray houndstooth and black leather dancing shoes into a charcoal merino tracksuit and moss nubuck sneakers and went for a long run under well-lit streets to burn off enough stress to fall asleep. It was his last night in New Growl. His business trip was done, and if future sojourns to New Growl were required, he wouldn't return to Dance-Dance. Tin was careful enough to treat dance halls like mistakes and never frequent the same one twice. He didn't go out to be remembered; he danced to forget. And fuck forgiveness—she was someone else's bitch.

Stars, seeing Bibi again had riled him up more than he thought. Tin picked up his pace, putting more distance between him and the past.

Far behind him, like the long tail of a disappointed comet, trailed a taxi with a steely-eared passenger.

Dressed in a comfortable glen plaid lounge suit with wide lapels for traveling, fur fluffed and precisely styled, Tin Silbursun-Howell was in a taxi on his way to the airport when he turned on his mobile and the barrage of notifications sent his phone into a dinging tizzy. Sent him into a fizzy tizzy, too, until he remembered his deep breathing exercises. Deep breath in... Slow breath out... Breathe in today... A blank slate awaits... Slowly breathe out yesterday... Goodbye to—

Tin's phone rang with an incoming call, interrupting his meditation. He didn't answer. The ringing stopped, then immediately started again.

"You wanna handle your business, Mr. Businesswolf?" The cabbie adjusted the rearview mirror and forced eye contact with Tin.

Her whiskers tsked and her snout crinkled in true mammalia rodentia disapproval. New Growl taxi rats were a tough bunch.

Tin faced his screen. It was his mother. He accepted the call and put the phone to his ear without speaking.

"Don't come here," she said and hung up.

Love you, too, he thought, and *This can't be good*. In deference to the cabbie, he didn't want his phone's meltdown to distract her as she squirreled in and out of traffic. He turned the volume

    WOLVES ALWAYS HOWL TWICE

off, then checked his text messages. It seemed everyone he knew sent a text, and the messages fell into two camps—mostly because the haters didn't have his new number (yet).

From his family (many): *Go to Paw City as planned.*

From his friends (few): *Got your flank, cuz.*

He scrolled through the news feeds and almost flinched at the trending topic: *Missing Mogul.* So much for letting yesterday go. His yoga instructor hadn't said what to do if yesterday tracked you down and screamed in your face. Tin shut down his phone without responding to a single text or returning any calls. Continued to the airport as planned. He did not, as planned, go to Paw City, however. And since he certainly couldn't stay in New Growl, he booked a ticket to Old Town.

It was all very well for his family to insist he tough it out, but he'd done that once and got kicked for it. This time, he was going to hide before reporters (and John Q. Public) remembered he existed. He cursed the day he said hello to the Nougattes. Like that poem about losing a war for want of a nail, Tin Silbur-sun-Howell bought a rising sport-star a drink, which ended a marriage, which tanked his career and ended in death (not his). Full of recriminations and busy trying to get the taste of bitter off his tongue, Tin never noticed the rabbit in a very rumpled suit three rows behind him on the flight.

B: Help! I don't know what to do.

B: Hello?

B: Where are you? Everything ok?

B: Call as soon as you get this! This is a nightmare!! Press everywhere!!!

B: We need to talk! You disappeared last night.

B: Please don't ignore me. Darling. I need to know.

From Old Town, Tin took a train north to the woods of Lake Forster, then used the car hire service meant for The ASH Lodge and Resort guests, because if he asked any of his relatives who knew how to drive for a lift, there was a good chance they'd instead pigeon-carry him back to the airport and frog-march him onto a Paw City-bound plane.

His driver, Pickles Olschewski—a dour-looking beaver who'd thumped Tin on more than one occasion growing up—pointed out the taxi following them, but Tin figured it was probably a reporter looking for a scoop and said as much.

Pickles replied, "Your grave, man." Which Tin took to mean Pickles disagreed.

The taxi turned at the resort's entrance while they continued through the forest, past the No Admittance signs and through the elaborate alder gate (carved by Pickles' grandmother) and was immediately forgotten by Tin. He was more concerned about the pack of nieces and nephews awaiting him in the den's front yard, clutching soccer balls.

"Really, Pickles? You messaged the family chat about ferrying me?"

"It's my job," the beaver said, and okay, technically yes, but give a guy a break.

"I'm not an official guest."

"It wasn't an official message. Get out of my car. I've real guests to get."

Tin exited and decided to delay, mayhap avoid, the discussion with his family about his return by supervising the kiddos.

They howled in glee when Tin undressed to his undershirt and wide-striped boxer shorts, despite the slight autumn chill, and they realized Uncle Tin wasn't going to *maybe next time* them or insist on being goalie or ref or coach but actually *play*. And as he ran up and down the field, giving pointers, letting them steal the ball from him, stealing it away when an older child took it off a younger player, he wondered why he'd denied himself the joy of playing the sport he loved. Standing on the sidelines, never fully participating.

He wasn't sure if he'd been trying to protect or punish himself; a sad attempt at being an adult? Or if he was simply trying to avoid the possibility of a stranger seeing his moves and recalling the scandal, reviving the gossip and sidelong glances. As if he didn't do anything too Tin Silbursun-Howell-like, if he erased the things that made him *him*, that the world would forget he existed and he could go about his days in anonymity. Which he had. And like all things, it worked until it didn't.

M: Traveling. Will return soon. With good news

At half past dawn, Tin jogged across the yard and into the woods. His brother Laqq had offered to accompany Tin on his morning run, but he left the house before his brother woke. None of the adults in the family were happy about his visit to Lake Forster (except maybe Aunt Hilde, who thrived on being bossy and riding to the rescue, so was thrilled to attend the Paw City meetings in Tin's stead). Especially Laqq, who complained at length about Tin not fulfilling his obligations to the family business, about Tin putting the family's name in a bad light, about Tin once again, until it went on so long their mother—

who heartily agreed with her son's litany—snapped at Laqq in annoyance. Tin hadn't wanted Laqq to pick up where he'd left off last night or join his mother at the breakfast table, so it was a solo morning run along the trails.

Tin was on his second loop with his ears pricked and an eye out for Laqq (who he expected to join him with a host of new complaints). Instead, Tin caught a flicker of color among the pines that didn't belong, and he slowed slightly for a better look. Contrary to his brother's claims, Tin didn't knowingly rush headlong into danger. Case in point: he had ducked out of the dance hall and returned to Lake Forster to avoid talking to Bibi, hadn't he? And that had been the right decision because the shadowy shape among the trees was none other than the wall-flower rabbit.

He took two more steps in the rabbit's direction, thinking he'd confront his unwanted shadow. Give them a *no comment* for the record when it occurred to Tin that the rabbit may not be there for a story, but for him. And while he was certain he was stronger of the two if the rabbit physically attacked him, a rabbit who followed a wolf all the way from New Growl to Lake Forster may have come prepared. Might be packing heat even. Either instinct or scent sent Tin's snout high into the air, and he let out a series of short *woo, woo, woos* followed by a frenzy of loud barks.

The chorus of answering barks and growls spooked the rabbit. Who turned tail and dashed off into the woods.

Laqq was the first to reach Tin's location and furiously tackled him to the ground, branches cracking beneath them. The broken end of a twig poked sharply into the meat of Tin's thigh.

"Ouch! What the comet, Laqq!"

"You don't stand there like a moony statue and let a nutjob shoot you, Tins."

Around the brothers, the woods echoed with warnings. The brothers got to their feet, and Tin shook his head to fling the debris from his fur, then picked at the burrs and sticks clinging to his tracksuit. Smoothed his fur into place.

"Did you even check for poison ivy or thistles before you knocked me over? Look, my pants are ripped, and my skin's scratched."

"Yet your head's still attached to your body, so Mom will thank me," Laqq said. "Why's a rabbit trying to kill you? Do we need to worry? Or is this about why you came scurrying home?"

"As you reminded me last night: not everything's about me. Could be a lost hiker. Or a hunter. A journalist carrying a pea shooter for protection. Doesn't mean they want me dead." Except he, the rabbit, and Bibi being at the same place, same time narrowed down the multiple potential reasons someone would come after Tin to one. And that mare would steeplechase you into the nearest pit and call it a grave.

"Sure, Tins. Whatever story you want to tell to make yourself feel better. What if the nutjob had gone after you yesterday while you were coaching the littles? Huh? Thought about that?"

"Point made, Laqq. I'll... handle it, all right?" Laqq did not look convinced. Truth told, Tin wasn't convinced himself. His track record for dealing with Bibi's machinations was deeply scratched and skipped when played.

Somewhat disheveled from their impromptu run through the woods, Mohair Eaves barged back into their hotel room, mentally packed and ready to retreat to New Growl. They could've headed straight to the train station and left their belongings behind, but Mohair needed their laptop—which was still in the rented room at Station House B&B. They were yanking their suitcase out of the closet when they spotted a wolf lounging in the low-slung, padded armchair in the room's far corner.

Tin Silbursun-Howell was here.

Waiting for them.

They froze, then spun about, luggage in hand. It'd pack a nice wallop if swung with sufficient force.

"Disconcerting, isn't it?" the wolf asked. "A familiar face in an unexpected place?"

He'd changed since their run-in in the woods and now wore a charcoal and white puppytooth suit, jacket unbuttoned, with a claret turtleneck (merino wool). He looked unbothered and sockdolager. Mohair—feeling ever the ragamuffin—stayed quiet, evaluating their options.

"Why are you following me?"

The wolf wanted answers? Ha! Mohair was here to demand explanations and issue deterrents. They'd ask the questions. "Where's Meret?" The wolf had the audacity to look confused. "Meret Nury! Bibi's husband! What did you do to him?" Mohair shouted.

"I can't figure how you and Bibi connect. You don't look flush enough to catch her attention. And if you didn't disappear the husband, then I guess you're the chump with a short shelf life. Run far and fast before you drown in her wake. So as long as I'm not in the frame..." The wolf stood, making eyes at the door.

Mohair stepped sideways to block his exit. "I saw the threats you sent Bibi."

"I don't make threats."

That sounded like it might be a threat. Mohair waited for the next line, *I make promises*. But the wolf didn't say anything else, just stood there, patient-like, waiting for Mohair to get out of his way.

"You think I'm scared of you?" Mohair said. "The big, bad wolf and the fluffy bunny?"

The wolf threw back his head, exposing his furry neck and guffawed. Mohair spotted a small, snagged burr tangled in the otherwise groomed fur. "You've got that backwards, champ. You're the big, bad bunny, and I'm the fluffy wolf."

Mohair didn't quite understand what was happening here. The wolf thought Mohair was the menace? They gave the wolf a twice-over. Silbursun-Howell displayed no aggression. Had called for help upon seeing Mohair in Lake Forster. Had run from Dance-Dance at the mere sight of Bibi like hounds nipped at his heels. Didn't even try to speak with her or ask the object of his unwanted affections for a dance. Could this conflict-ducking, egalitarian ballroom Oliver Twist have done all the things Bibi claimed?

Ruined her marriage?

Driven her first husband to suicide?

Stalked her? (While living in a different town and traveling everywhere but New Growl...)

Abducted and/or murdered Meret? (While Mohair had been tailing him...)

Doubt wiggled in. "You are kinda fluffy."

"The fluffiest," Tin agreed. "Look— What's your name?"

"Mohair Eaves."

"Look, Eaves. My bet is one—or both—of the Nurys has a sweetheart. It's not me. Maybe Bibi found someone with more dough than Hubby No. 2 to be Hubby No. 3. Or Mr. Missing Mogul regrets tying himself to a controlling snake, but isn't willing to take the dead way out. Not with other, warmer options out there, yeah? And Moon knows, there are plenty of people with reasons to want me dead. But I don't think you're one of them. So—" The wolf held up a finger. "—if that's not *your* gun in your pocket, if Bibi gave it to you, and you truly don't know what happened to her current husband—think about it. That gun's probably what disappeared Mr. Missing Mogul.

Do you really want to go down for two murders? No one may know what happened to the husband... yet... But plenty of people witnessed you and me, yeah? At Dance-Dance? In the woods just now? They find that stallion's body, match the bullets to that gun... see where this is going? Don't be the nice, neat little bow the cops use to wrap up these crimes."

Mohair felt it burning a hole in their pocket—Bibi had loaned them the revolver. Could the wolf be right? Shuck a duck. "And I should believe you, why? You bit Mackinaw Nougatte. During that game. You blaming Bibi for that, too? He killed himself."

Tin sighed. Rubbed the fur on his cheeks, making it even fluffier. "Having 'fangs' doesn't make me a killer. Mackie is not dead because I'm a wolf. Mackie is dead because he and Bibi liked to party, and he liked the booze and drugs more than was good for him. It affected his play. It was going to affect his pay, *and* it made him crazy-jelly. Bibi was sneaking around on him— probably with that slick stallion. But Bibi and I were never a thing. Mackie and I were never a thing. They asked; I declined. We were briefly friends. I make a convenient scapegoat. Because of that mucking clip. Which, if you haven't watched the full game, you should. And if you have any 'predator' friends: watch with them. Ask what they see. Because I never even broke that stinkin' onion's skin!" He took a step toward the door, into Mohair's personal space. "Are you going to do Bibi's dirty work and shoot me?"

Mohair was still trying to process the implications of the wolf's words and fit them into the puzzle they thought they'd already solved. Their ears rested against their back, either in atavistic relaxation or embarrassment.

"You're not what I expected."

"If it's any consolation, I didn't expect you at all." Tin Silbur-sun-Howell slunk around Mohair; a mere scrape of fabric against fabric as he left. Before the door clicked shut, he added, "Bibi's sticky like glue. She'll make a mess of you, too."

Mohair had a ton more questions, but decided not to chase after a wolf. They had some self-preservation.

Instead, they heaved the suitcase—still clutched in their right hand—up onto the bed and began packing, with a side of plotting.

M: Problem solved. Invoice attached.

Blind spots. Even rabbits have them. Mohair had to concede that rich people's problems might require the kind of solutions they didn't want to specialize in. They'd been so focused on strategies to discourage Tin Silbursun-Howell, they didn't thoroughly scan the entire meadow before chowing down on clover.

They failed to verify their client's claims, knowing full well that clients usually colored the truth, oft times lied.

They failed to consider other candidates for prowlers.

They failed to prevent Meret Nury's disappearance, possibly death.

They failed. Spectacularly.

Luckily, jumping to conclusions wasn't the only leap in logic Mohair had left in 'em. The messages Bibi received could have come from Bibi herself. Meret Nury had dismissed his wife's worries. Bibi had referred to the wolf as Tinny— A pet name for someone who was stalking you? In hindsight, that was odd. And, come to think, she'd said the police *wouldn't* do anything, not confirmed that she actually filed a report. Mohair should've checked, got a copy, confirmed that the cops were useless instead of assuming it. Meret Nury was a big deal in New Growl. The idea that he couldn't bankroll his influence to get the cops to do his bidding... At least they hadn't shot Tin Silbursun-Howell.

Mohair made a few side trips before returning to New Growl, including one to West Chirrup to ensure the Char-Ashs hadn't been joined by a trussed-up stallion. They hadn't. So, not kidnapping accomplices. However, even briefly observing the jackal and the large-eared, foxy-looking borochi, Mohair noticed mannerisms peculiar to the Lake Forster Silbursun-Howells and speculated this might be a crooked branch on the family's tree (which intrigued them all the more.) They would've surveilled longer, but judging by the frequent and borderline frantic texts Mohair wasn't answering, a client eagerly awaited their return. They dropped a package off addressed to The ASH Group c/o Char-Ashs ATTN: Tin and split.

Mohair arranged to meet Bibi at Halya's. They were tempted to go to the Nougatte-Nury house (Bibi's suggestion) but decided meeting in public was better. It was unlikely Meret Nury was hidden on his own property and, after checking the police had searched the residence and gardens, insisted on the tea shop—home field advantage and all.

No zebra was Mohair's first thought on entering Halya's Teas & Leaves.

They called out, "Hello?", and Halya himself appeared from the back room with a scowl. "Where's your brasseur?" Mohair asked, also noticing the lack of patrons, but tables still topped with cups and saucers and used serviettes—a rare sight which nettled Mohair's nerves.

"Missing."

That startled Mohair. "Missing?"

"No, no. Not *missing* like you go find. *Missing* like not come to work." Halya also seemed to notice the empty tables needing bussing. "I had client. No time to clean after rush. I make your tea. Then clean. You want reading, too? You look like you need some fortune."

A thumping sound came from the back. Like, Mohair thought, the sound of someone trying to break in—or out. Was Halya holding Bibi hostage? No, Mohair was letting the stress of everything make them jumpy. They'd expected... not a crowd but a witness or three. At least they weren't carrying around the revolver anymore. Mohair wasn't sure if sending it to Tin Silbursun-Howell was inspired or batty.

"This is a bad time. I'll—"

Just then the bell announced a customer, and Bibi Nougatte-Nury strode in, blocking their retreat. She wore a beige silk dress with a cartwheel hat that cast half her face in shadow and gripped her sequined clutch like a rock she wanted to bash over their head.

"Is it done?" she demanded, and Mohair was quick to note she no longer looked in need of help. They tested their theory.

"Everything's fixed. That wolf won't bother you again. Was Meret found?" Because a missing spouse was certainly worthy of a hitch or two in one's step. Unless one's spouse was the problem, then his being gone would clear that right up.

"Tin killed Meret. You have to know that. Do you still have my insurance? Or is it settled?"

She meant the gun. She'd tucked it into Mohair's pocket outside Dance-Dance, and whispered, *You never know when you might need a little insurance to cover your assets.*

Mohair flicked their awareness behind them to study Halya, who stood between them and a quick exit out of the back and didn't seem perturbed by talk of murder and insurance. *Insurance.* Mohair wanted to thump themself on the forehead for never considering that Bibi might be a black widow looking to gild her web. Too dazzled by Bibi's sunshine-y reflective glow to spot her rotten undercoat.

They sidestepped between two tables to avoid being squashed in a Halya-Bibi acorn sandwich.

"You bring my money?" Mohair asked.

"Tell me about the gun, darling," Bibi said. "Then you'll get your money. Where is it?"

"Meret isn't going to be found, is he? Who shot him for you? Your boyfriend?"

Halya sighed, dipping his horn. "I told you: smart bunny. Funny, yes, but quick. They do the puzzles. Simpler plan would've been better."

That wasn't who they expected to be in cahoots with Bibi, and Mohair realized their plan was goose -cooked.

Hubby No. 3, Mohair thought. *Awesome.*

"Zip it," Bibi said. "This can still work. Having the gun would be diamonds, but coal burns, too."

Mohair wasn't waiting around for the couple to decide their fate. They skedaddled—or tried to. Their shoe caught on a chair leg, and they crashed into a table, hands first. Dishware rattled, and instinctively, Mohair steadied them to keep them from dashing to bits, thought better of it, and threw a cup at Bibi. Flung its saucer like a discus at Halya. As artillery went, spoiled vegetables were better.

Mohair hoisted a chair to use as a shield or toss; they hadn't decided.

The teacup hit Bibi on the length of her face, but she startled more from the dregs splashing her. The saucer bounced off Halya's upper arm, and he responded with a guttural bellow, lowering his head to charge at Mohair. His growl almost drowned out the sound of the shop's bell. Almost.

They stilled.

In unison, their heads turned to see a stately businesswolf in a royal blue cutaway coat and silk striped trousers enter the shop using an ebony cane. Her fur had the alpine white glint of age, and she looked the type to fleece the other grande dames at Vanderbleet's bridge in a 'friendly' game.

"Is this where you read leaves?" She peered over her pince-nez eyeglasses at the splatter on the honeycomb-tiled floor. "I rather thought you'd read them in the cup. How delightful! Tell me, what do they signify?" She gazed at Mohair. "Well, are you going to simply hold that chair or bring it over so I can sit? And you—" She flicked her cane at Bibi to move her aside. "—will need to do something about those stains. Some beading. Or maybe a floral appliqué. Are you one of those fancy fringe and geo-whatsits artists deco? Doesn't matter. I know a fabulous needleworker. A porcupine. None better." She stamped her cane twice. "The chair, please!"

"What," shrieked Bibi, "are you talking about? Get out!"

"Hormones are terrible, aren't they? You'll feel better after a visit to the ladies'. Go on. Splash some water on you."

Mohair picked their way over to the door and set the chair next to her. "You—"

Before Mohair could utter another word, Halya recovered.

"Madam. Madam. Please." He held his arms wide. "We are not at our best. If you could—"

Madam sat. "What is it you do here? Make tea? I'll have one. With gin. Milk makes me gassy."

"—really should go," Mohair continued."These ungulates—"

"Another time, madam. If you would—"

"Give me the gun! Give it to me!" Bibi kicked the counter.

"—come back tomorrow, I'd gladly read your leaves then. The shop isn't—"

"Is it because of the naked zebra wandering around outside?"

Halya did a double-take of the back room and the front window and the back door again.

"Don't fret. I called the police. They'll sort things out. If you don't have gin, just brew me something with juniper. Can you read berries?" The businesswolf addressed Mohair, ignoring Bibi as if she were a toddler throwing a tantrum and would soon tire herself out.

Mohair cupped the woman's elbow and urged her to her feet. "Maybe tomorrow would be better? You could bring your own gin. I can walk you out."

She stayed roosted where she was. "That's a 'no' on the berries, then?"

"I don't do the readings. He's the tasseographer." Mohair tilted their head toward Halya, who looked as perplexed as a platypus. They took comfort that no one's plan was working out the way they thought. Not even the businesswolf could pick her poison.

"Ah!" She gave a wide, wolfy smile, revealing capped canines. That made her older than they'd guesstimated. A great grande dame. "Then *you* must be the detective."

Mohair's hand fell away from her arm. She was a Silbursun-Howell!

"We really should leave," they said. "They're criminals."

"I know," she said. "I'm Tin's Aunt Hilde. The police are coming for them."

"No one's getting arrested—except maybe Eavesey. They killed your nephew. And my husband."

Bibi's stories didn't sound convincing anymore. Maybe she was losing her sparkle.

Aunt Hilde harrumphed. "All your husbands may be dead,

but my nephews are still howling. Didn't Eaves tell you? They cottoned to your scheme and bobbed your tail good."

"That's a laugh." Bibi pulled a lipstick out of her clutch and reapplied.

Halya pulled out a chair and sank down onto it.

Aunt Hilde stretched her neck and let out a surprisingly full-bodied howl. It mingled with the wail of the police cars rushing their way.

Then, from close by, came an answering howl. Mohair recognized it as Tin's. It was a distinctly fluffy-sounding howl.

Aunt Hilde looked triumphant. "It's the second Howell that gets you," she said, and Mohair bet the lady had that printed on visiting cards.

Mohair chanced a peek out the window. "Is there really a naked zebra?"

"As a jaybird. And proud as a peacock about it. You can have a looksee."

Mohair demurred, but Halya got up and stuck his large head out the door for a gander. Mohair wondered if the rhino'd make a run for it, but he didn't. He watched for a few, then opened the door wider and let the officers in.

"Thank you for coming," he said. "We've had some disturbance."

The basset cop scanned the room, taking in the broken ceramics and spilt tea, the occupants of the tea room.

The pronghorn asked, "How'd this happen?"

Bibi stretched her arm out, pointing at Mohair. "That rabbit's a killer!"

Everyone eyed Mohair, whose fur was extra curly due to some earlier flop sweating.

They brushed their curls back, and gave their best sheep's eyes. "That's Bibi Nougatte-Nury. Her second husband's missing, and she's not handling it well. I think she might hurt herself. She asked me for a gun."

"She did this." Aunt Hilde gestured with her cane. "Didn't like her reading and threw a fit. Came out kicking at the counter like a stabled horse. You can see the scuff marks match her shoes."

The basset studied the black smudges, then Bibi's shoes. "Did you kick this counter?"

"They're taking everything out of context! Halya, tell them!"

"What was the reading?" the pronghorn said.

"There was no reading!"

The basset asked, "Who owns this place?"

"I do!" Bibi screeched.

"Is that true?" the basset asked Halya.

The rhino looked at Bibi for a long moment. The cops moved to corral her, if necessary.

Then Halya spoke. "This is my place. Halya's Tea and Leaves. I'm Halya. She's a Bibi."

"How do you know her?"

"As a client. I am a gifted tasseographer. I read the best fortunes. She wanted to know if her husband would be found. She asked about insurance. Diamonds. I did not see those things in the cup."

"And the gun?"

"Are you actually doing this?" Bibi said.

"She did say, 'Give me the gun. Give it to me.' Maybe she hurt herself. But there is no gun to give. Then the cups and saucers break, everything is chaos."

Bibi read the room. She wiped at her eyes as if they were welling up. "Maybe I am a little distraught. My head's a little mixed up. I—I might need some help. Do you think you could help me?"

"Let's get you to the hospital." The pronghorn and the basset gently bracketed Bibi to escort her from the tea shop.

On her way out, she asked, "Aren't you forgetting something?" The cops looked at each other, then at her. "The naked zebra? How do you think she got so loopy? Halya's the go-to for cat's meow. Maybe someone should take a looksee in his storeroom."

The pronghorn got on the radio and called for another set of officers to come in and cuff Halya. As soon as he was tucked in the back of the police car, a zebra with a bobbed mane and long legs came in wearing nothing but an overcoat and shook her head at the mess.

"Bibi'll be out in three," Aunt Hilde predicted.

"Days?" Mohair said, thinking that was probably long enough for Bibi to catch herself a rich doctor.

"Hours."

"Minutes," the zebra said, grabbing an empty tray, collecting the discarded dishware. "You see how she was cozying up to that pronghorn? They might let her out at the next traffic light."

"And Halya?" Mohair asked.

"Oh, he won't be back," the zebra said, and Aunt Hilde agreed. "See how the leaves on the tiles curve into angry little horseshoes? That's a stampede."

GORILLIANAIRE

ANGELIQUE O'ROURKE

Hildebrand carefully pulls on each glove and straightens her matching hat. Glancing in the mirror for confirmation that the outfit looks as she wishes it, she retrieves her handbag from the hook on the wall and walks out the door.

A call from Drummond at any hour would have been concerning. But at 6 am, the only options were an emergency or the rare call on the depressing, drunken tail end of an all-nighter.

"... Hello?" She'd answered hesitantly, having woken only moments before.

"Hildebrand—" Drummond was whispering, the oddness of which quickened her pulse in alarm. "Something's happened. I... I don't know how to explain. I didn't know who to call. Can you come here?"

"Where are you? At the condo in Ham Hock?"

"Shit, no, we haven't been in touch. I'm on the island. Can you make it to the airstrip? I'll send my plane."

Hildebrand was harried and off-balance. "You want me to go to the private airport and meet you in the Bahamas, right now?"

Drummond exhaled in an aggrieved, shaky way. "Yes, I know I sound insane. Please, just... I can't stay on this line long. I don't know who's listening. Ugh, just, can you come?" He sounded near tears, which alarmed her even further.

"Um, yes. Yeah. I can just move some work stuff around on my way. Sit tight."

Drummond was actually crying lightly. She could tell by his breathing. "Thank you. Thank you." He gave her the flight details and hung up.

That was about an hour ago, and Hildebrand has been in crisis management mode since. Showering, packing (she didn't ask how long the stay would be and didn't want to call back, something felt too raw—she just took enough things for about a long weekend and knew she could manage for longer if needed), and sending some emails to let clients know she had a family emergency.

A family emergency, the nature of which is unknown, but the tenor of which is both bizarre and frightening. Her older brother and she are not close; they had been as children though, which gave them a sort of permanent shorthand with each other. An emotional direct line of communication. There's a specific type of access to someone else that comes only with having interacted with them on a regular basis while growing up; nothing else can emulate it. In any case, Drummond has never reached out like this before. He could be messy, but more of a melancholy, pontificating playboy messy than a desperate plea for company messy.

Briskly walking down the street to her car parked on the corner, she has genuinely no idea what she's heading into.

Cockatiel Heights is her favorite neighborhood in New Growl, bustling but not overrun with foot traffic, vaguely artsy while remaining primarily residential. She feels at home here, and often reflects on her good fortune to be an animal who has largely felt at home in the world from the start. The city's name has always caused her to crack a wry smile, though. As a gorilla, even the bipedal and straight-backed version they'd evolved into, she thinks to herself, *if I know one thing for certain, we don't growl—we roar.*

    GORILLIANAIRE

When she and Drummond were little, they had an easy rapport. He was charming and rakish; she was earnest, stoic, and somewhat prim. By chance, their personalities fit fairly naturally into the roles expected of them by their well-to-do, reserved family. They weren't the best of friends, but the house was harmonious, and privilege held hardship far out of sight and mind.

As they came of age, they grew apart. Hildebrand was always drawn to the practical things in life. Not at the expense of pleasure—she wasn't ascetic, but becoming a forensic accountant was enough excitement for her day-to-day life. Drummond thrived on risk and competition, which Hildebrand found exhausting and more than a little shallow.

Over time, he became obsessed with growing the modest wealth he had access to into a sort of grotesque treasure pile in a dragon's cave, hoarding for hoarding's sake, showing off and grandstanding. Hildebrand kept her distance. She didn't understand the draw or the point. He'd built a cult of personality around himself, using his sparkle to draw in a perpetual entourage of admirers, invariably animals that Hildebrand could find no conversational footholds among. It was all so cliché. Drummond had written a memoir (with accompanying podcast and YouTube channel, of course) called 'Gorillianaire', for Christ's sake. How could you not laugh and shake your head, at least a little?

The flight to Exuma takes a little less than 3 hours.

After the decline of humans, the Exuma swimming pigs moved on from Big Major Cay into the rest of the islands and now handle all of the tourism from other animals and the general upkeep. It's a beautiful and restful place.

Hildebrand has been fortunate to visit Drummond a

handful of times over the years. He lives on the island part-time, with a glamorous pig named Samra that Hildebrand has seen in photos but never met.

During the flight, she wonders idly if Samra will be there when she arrives.

When Hildebrand opens the door to the private residence on the island, it's dim and shaded inside. The heat of the day is masked with chilly AC, and all of the window coverings are drawn.

Drummond is sitting on the floor on a plush white rug, his back resting against the leather sofa. He has several devices spread about him in a semi-circle: tablets, phones, a laptop, something that looks like a walkie-talkie or a satellite phone. His face is drawn and ashen.

"Hi," he says, with a quavering, ironic smile. "Long time no see."

"Hey," Hildebrand replies. "What am I looking at right now?" She gestures to the tech strewn across the floor. "Are you having some kind of AV Club seance?"

Drummond chuckles weakly. "Oh yeah, I'm summoning the ghost of my dead career." He grimaces. "Okay. I don't really know where to start here. This morning, I mean. I know this had to have been planned well beyond this morning, but this is when I discovered it. This morning I went to check on some accounts, and things were not right—not just not right, but deeply fucked, actually. Multiple high-balance accounts had been completely emptied. Not a fucking clue where that money was routed. Just gone. And not just that, but when I looked into my crypto, most of it's fine, but some of it has also been transferred out." The way he says that last phrase is very strange in tone, almost as if he's afraid to continue speaking. He picks up his crypto cold storage wallet and hands it to her.

"Transferred out of your account and into whose?" Hildebrand asks. Drummond looks at her balefully.

"This is why I called you." He swallows hard. "I need you to believe that I did not willingly do this. Alright? I did not choose this—this is fucking thievery. Okay?"

Hildebrand sits on the other sofa facing him.

"Okay. The more information I have, the easier it will be for me to parse out what happened." She assures him.

He continues in a quaver. "Transferred to... bad people. I recognize some groups because they have approached me before, and I've turned it down, but... I don't know, I don't know if someone betrayed me or it's just hackers or what the fuck, but as of this morning it looks like I've transferred funds to crypto accounts associated with organized crime. Terrorists, gangs, mafias."

"Which means we're talking drugs, animal trafficking, arms smuggling, and money laundering," Hildebrand supplies.

Drummond looks physically sick. He makes eye contact with her. "Hundreds of millions."

She takes a deep, measured breath. This is an absolute shitshow.

Hildebrand and Drummond's parents were professionals from upper middle class families who had received inheritances from their own parents and managed their money well. They gave each of their children a trust of a million dollars at age 18. Hildebrand used the money for college tuition and to live on during college and several years beyond while she built her small accounting practice. She put a down payment on a home in a nice neighborhood of New Growl, leased a favorably positioned office space in the city as well, and owned a reliable car.

Also, let's be honest, she used it to construct a smart wardrobe of tailored dresses, suits, kitten-heeled shoes, matching coats, hats and gloves. Maybe it was an indulgence, but she was proud of her sense of style and her vintage-inspired, feminine outfits. She liked to look and feel put together.

Hildebrand, sitting at her desk back in Cockatiel Heights, cracks her knuckles at her desk before getting to work.

The first task is a bit of light time travel. *Animals haven't completely cracked it with time travel,* she thinks to herself, *but as far as history tells us, humans never figured it out at all, so we're at least a few steps ahead.* Time travel in actuality is much different from how it was portrayed in old human popular media—the crux of it being that it's a bit of an invisible man situation.

Turns out the butterfly effect wasn't the world's biggest concern after all, because what you're really doing is witnessing the past. You can not alter it. The past is visible like a film that one stands in, unnoticed—reminiscent of a VR headset. For reasons animals have yet to decipher completely, the future is not available in this manner. The working theory is that while the past has already occurred, and thus is at least somewhat linear up to the present moment, the future is constantly being created from a multitude of possibilities within the present moment. There aren't any linear strains to follow.

Time travel into the past also isn't easy on the body. Current tech lets animals go back as far as three months (work is ever-occurring to try and increase that span—the first machines only did one week), but that makes the traveler a little ill for a while afterward. Like an extreme form of jet lag. And it eats up some time in the present. Every trip to the past is more or less like sleeping—you're simply sitting in the time machine's thrall for the duration of your travel and 'wake up' just sitting in the same position, with the equivalent amount of time having passed in the present. There are already animals, usually the recently bereaved, whiling days away lost in a loop of replaying recent memories.

For today's particular task, Hildebrand calibrates her home office time machine for the date of the first sketchy transaction she finds. It's only for $20, but that's often how these scams work. There are a few test balloons, a very slow trickle that will fly unnoticed as proof of concept to the hackers, and then— boom. The 'boom' in this case, the high-value coordinated thefts, was on April 22nd, two days ago.

The time machine drops her into Drummond's Ham Hock neighborhood office around the start of the business day. Ham Hock is the slick, chrome and glass condo filled business district of New Growl, its moniker an ironic reclaiming of a gruesome human practice and a nod to the proud brutality of the capitalist culture there. Drummond, of course, has an enormous corner office complete with the Gorillianaire podcast set up.

8 am, one month ago, not much was going on. Drummond sat at his desk, looking at his screen with a furrowed brow. Hildebrand turns her device forward a few days, skimming through time like a fast forward button so it only takes a few seconds in real time —stops when she sees what looks like an argument.

When she drops back into the scene, there is a strung-out kangaroo angrily spitting out the sentence, "Then make it look above board!"

Drummond glowered. "Alright, christ. I'll handle it."

The kangaroo's body language eased a bit. "Teddy will be happy to hear that. We appreciate you."

Confused, Hildebrand runs back a bit to try and catch the beginning of the argument, but... ugh. The timeline has been blurred. Time travel tech is still in its infancy and, unsurprisingly, there are many animals who benefit from others not being able to see for themselves what actually happened in the past.

Timeline-blurring devices have cropped up that crudely obscure the past from view and hearing—essentially distorting the sounds and images beyond comprehension, as if you're in a smeared painting listening to unintelligible muffled sounds.

She comes back to the present in her office. *Well, the fact that this section was blurred is useful data,* she thinks. It tells her that the kangaroo either had something to do with the theft, or is generally shady and hiding something.

She uses a still of the haggard kangaroo from the argument to search through images from New Growl news segments and articles; she only gets one hit, but it's the only one she needs. The kangaroo is walking in an entourage through a swarm of press outside of a courthouse, behind several people being brought up on RICO charges a few years ago—a case that got dismissed. One of the defendants, an unnervingly muscular kangaroo jack, is Theodore Alexander, a billionaire CEO of a private security firm with links to just about every stripe of large-scale organized crime imaginable. Hildebrand groans out loud when she sees his face. She's met this guy before. It's Drummond's friend Teddy.

The pieces start falling into place as she follows the money, looking for any connections to Teddy, Drummond or either of their companies. There's a sudden rush of realization and adrenaline when it occurs to her that April 22nd is when many humans used to celebrate something they called 'Earth Day', a day to advocate for the health of the planet and combat climate change. It has taken on the dark tone of a cautionary tale since their decline.

Climate change was significantly stymied but is slowly ramping up again with the accelerating evolution of animals the world over. Pulling on that thread, Hildebrand discovers that the accounts that stole the money are loosely linked to various environmental conservation groups (all, of course, located in countries with no extradition treaties and no real interest in cooperating with New Growl law enforcement) and to Shadow, a sort of Robinhood-esque hacking group with members in the wind that could be anywhere, a successor to what the humans did with the historical group Anonymous. *Okay,* she thinks, *we've got an illegal redistribution of wealth situation on our hands.*

But something is off. Why was Drummond making this sound like the money was stolen by the world's biggest bad guys? Looking over the transfers, it was mostly taken by vigilantes (for causes she found ultimately just, but still) and almost all on that same day.

Further back, however, at one point a few weeks before, Drummond's accounts had been recipients of huge deposits. The deposits constituted the bulk of what was stolen. These accounts are all associated with either one of two shell companies—not unusual for banking at this level. What is unusual is that the shell companies seem to have no legitimate business purpose she can suss out, and the accounts have made no direct purchases, only these large deposits, followed by some substantial transfers and withdrawals, before the hacking that emptied the accounts completely. Now, those *prior* transfers and withdrawals went down the rabbit hole to some bad shit. They are the first things Hildebrand look into chronologically, and they lead to exactly what Drummond said—a lot of dark money. But what she can find is cartels, drugs, and gun running; nightmare territory. But that was weeks ago. If that money was stolen by those groups, then why would more, albeit much smaller, subsequent deposits have been made? Why didn't he contact her earlier? How could Drummond have been so careless with this much money?

Her blood runs cold. He wasn't careless. He wasn't having her investigate the previous thefts because they weren't thefts. They were investments. Until the anomalous activity on April 22nd. They were expected transfers and withdrawals, because the money wasn't stolen by them. It was stolen *from* them. These were intended to be their accounts. Her memory jumps back to the time travel conversation she'd caught just a snippet of; this is what Drummond meant when he said he'd handle making it all look above board. And truthfully, if he didn't need her to find out the source of the vigilante hacking thefts, it would've continued to work.

Back at Drummond's house in Exuma later that evening, Hildebrand scoffs as it all clicks in her mind.

"So the emotion on the phone was real—only you were worried about covering your ass, not the nefarious uses of the money. All of the hand-wringing about organized crime and terrorism was for show to get me on board, because you knew I'd find those links too when I dug into this."

"If by covering my ass you mean trying not to get actually fucking murdered by some very pissed off and dangerous creatures, then yes. Excuse me for being animal. Even billionaires have emotions. Look, I'm sorry, Hilde. This has been a mess. I was terrified. I roped you into it all because I knew you had expertise I didn't, and we had to find out who did this to get the money back. And... if I'm being honest, because you're family, and I know you won't turn me in."

She lets this sit unchallenged. It's true.

"But it's over, okay? Now we can get the money to its rightful place, no one will be any the wiser that you were involved at all, and we can just put this behind us."

His smarmy self-assuredness is deeply grating to Hildebrand, even as he describes what was, to him, a high-stress situation as it unfolded. Now he's back on the familiar turf of expecting absolutely no resistance from anyone around him, that it's a complete given that what he says goes.

"No." The word just sort of arrives in Hildebrand's mouth of its own accord. But as soon as she says it, she knows it is what she means.

She won't turn in her own flesh and blood. She can't. She also won't be passing on the names of the hacking group or organizations she's uncovered, and she won't be participating in the retrieval of that money. The crypto wallet, still containing tens of millions of dollars of money from god knows what, just waiting to be laundered, remains back in New Growl on her desk.

Drummond bares his teeth and begins pacing, beside himself. A few times he leans forward, and she knows he is resisting the urge to gallop around the room on his knuckles in frustration.

"What in the fuck do you mean 'no'?" he barks. "You're a rule follower. You know stealing is wrong!"

A word very softly escapes Hildebrand's mouth as she tips her head to study her white eyelet spring gloves. "Wrong?"

The ensuing silence expands.

She contemplates how personal and private property laws are a human construct that didn't even exist until well after the agricultural revolution more than ten thousand years ago and how that continued on, exacerbated destruction, especially after the industrial revolution, and contributed to the eventual extinction of humans and the near extinction of their own species. She thinks of how, as time has rolled on, animals have evolved exponentially more quickly than they did previously, for reasons that are unclear even to themselves. But regardless, here we are. Just another group of primates with language, material culture—all of the things from the ancient texts marked 'Anthropology'. *We too are people, of our own distinction. And we don't have to make the same endless mistakes.*

"Wrong like staging thefts to save face when you actually are willingly funding these organizations and then hiring your sister to do a blind proxy investigation of the subsequent real thefts from them? Wrong like that? Making me what, an unwitting mafia PI? And for what? To crassly add yet more money to your giant pile of money? Or wrong like consistently overestimating your intelligence and abilities so much you sincerely thought I wouldn't figure that out even though *that is my fucking job?*"

"You're so fucking self-righteous. I bet you've been shelling out for the least of these right and left your entire life, right? Just like Jesus and Buddha, giving away all your worldly goods to charity."

Drummond rolls his eyes, his tone caustic.

"I don't give away all of my money, obviously, I'm wearing a suit from New Growl Fashion Week," she snaps impatiently. "But I do give away 30% of my income, after taxes. I have more than enough." She sighs, finds herself reaching forward almost as if to take his hand, though his broad desk is in the space between them. Her voice softens with familiarity. "We were so lucky, Drummond. We work hard of course, but we started on third base. How you've never understood that is beyond me."

He's looking at her with an expression that takes her a few seconds to register because it seems so out of place, but then it clicks: pity. She's just described the part of her life she's the most proud of, and he's looking at her like she's a stupid sucker. *God, what on earth must it be like inside your mind?* she wonders. But honestly, she's glad she can't imagine it.

"Jesus Drummond, don't you think at all that we should do it differently? That animals were given our chance for a reason, primates especially? All you aspire to be is some kind of human facsimile? You are *a* smart animal—not *the* smartest animal, not the *only* smart animal. From where I'm sitting with a courtside view of your life, much of what you have comes as a result of simple cruelty and a willingness to be the worst man in the room or have everyone around you hate you as long as they toe the line, rather than anything approaching smarts. Though I suspect you actually think that's all the same thing. Will you ever snap out of it and care about the wellbeing of other people?" She knows if she were literally any other animal in the world, he wouldn't have let her say any of this.

"I will; I *do*!" It's a snarl, a plea, and an obvious lie.

"You already could have a hundred times over," Hildebrand extends her arms out, palms up, in a gesture of exasperation. "25,000 animals die from starvation every day. It would cost around 7 billion to change that. I don't have that kind of money, but you *do*. You could have saved lives! You still can save some! Why are you so certain that everyone else should allow you to hoard resources like this?"

She knows she's laying into him in such a way that he's completely shut down. She sounds pedantic even to herself, but it's just rushing out. A sort of desperate cry into the abyss. She has the wild, ragged feeling that this might be the last time they ever speak to each other. The responsibility she feels to at least try to get through to him is overwhelming.

Drummond is furiously staring out the window, his back almost completely turned on her, and he'd taken out his phone partway through her diatribe.

"Yes, yes, I'm effectively a murderer, and I won't be able to take all my riches to hell with me," he lilts softly, scrolling. "Been great to see you, Sis, by the way." There's a whoosh sound from his device. "I just used my blood money to settle up the fee for your time. You know, since everyone so graciously *allows* me to have it." His voice is flat and steely.

Cringing, Hildebrand simply stands there, finally out of words.

At this, appearing to her like a ridiculous scene in a film, Drummond moves away from her decisively, wordlessly crossing to press a button behind his desk. Three hulking gorillas appear menacingly in the doorway, all looking to him for instruction.

Incredulous, Hildebrand raises her hands in the still-universal gesture of surrender and says, "I'll go, I'll go. There's no need for this."

She turns and starts towards the door, the security gorillas forming a loose circle formation around her until she is off of the property entirely, through the controlled gate.

On the hot sidewalk, she has that surreal, hollowed-out feeling of the aftermath of a moment that has changed her life's trajectory. She looks around her, mind casting about for the next step.

"He kick you out?" asks a stylish Bahamian pig who's slowly ambling up the sidewalk. Her voice has a lovely warm, round sound. She's wearing a dress of flowy, draped fabric and espadrilles.

"Um, yes. You know him?" Hildebrand replies, a little surprised.

She inclines her head toward Hildebrand, who suddenly recognizes her. "I'm Samra. He's been texting me. He's pretty pissed at you." She chuckles.

"Yeah, well. I'm pretty disappointed in him." Hildebrand responds.

"I was planning to drop in on him just now, but I think you and I should take a walk, maybe get a drink together," Samra offers.

Over drinks at a picturesque oceanside bar, a shellshocked Hildebrand ill-advisably spills the tea. She's just at a loss to understand his behavior. Samra shakes her head and stares out at the horizon. "You know, we've been together for many years, and in a way, I love him. It is bizarre, though. Because I genuinely don't know if he's capable of love in the way other people are. It is clear he wants me around, that he prefers my company. He seems to respect you, or at least, have a soft spot of caring for your opinion." She looks at Hildebrand meaningfully. "Both of those things are very rare among this kind of man. Maybe it qualifies as love."

Hildebrand sighs.

"In the face of all of this, I'm not even sure if that matters." Samra looks thoughtful. "Maybe it doesn't. But it might make you the only animal who can put at least some of this right."

When Samra tells her the passkey to the crypto cold storage wallet still sitting on her desk, Hildebrand asks her to repeat it. Not because she needs to memorize the number, but just out of surprise. It's one she already knows by heart.

Back at home, she holds his device in front of her. Incredibly, she enters the street address of their childhood home. And she's in.

Pulling the stand collar of her full-length, chocolate brown cashmere trench higher around her neck against the chilly breeze and light drizzle of a quickly darkening spring evening, Hildebrand's heels clack the streets of Cockatiel Heights some-what aimlessly to clear her head.

Is it a crime to donate the rest of that money? Legally, yes. But she knows Drummond can't really come after her because the money wasn't legally obtained to begin with; it's the same reason he won't be able to hire another forensic accountant to find out who stole it until he can find one corrupt enough to be paid off for turning a blind eye. Which, she's sure, he will, and in the not too distant future. And while she's confident he won't personally seek vengeance against her, Teddy and his cronies certainly could. But they could do that either way, simply because of her refusal to help. It's a sort of inverse Pascal's wager, where the stakes are many ordinary people's lives being greatly improved, at a few bad people's very minor expense.

What happens in her own life remains to be seen.

Contrary to what Drummond said earlier, she isn't and has never been an uncritical rule-follower. She's a meticulous animal with her own moral compass and risk tolerance, which is something else entirely. She's also been at this awhile and knows how to cover her own tracks.

She had already transferred it all that morning.

 GORILLIANAIRE

EMBOSSED IN IVY

BEN CURL

The Tale of Jacco M. Guus
By Ben Curl

I, Lepidoktera, in my endless pursuit to understand the civilizations and species that have preceded us, have recovered these relics of the lost city, New Growl. What they mean, I cannot say, but I can tell you what they are and how I obtained them.

Item A appears to be a diary entry. Two things make it unusual in comparison with the typical findings of the New Growl site. First, it was not written on paper but chiseled across a large cement slab. Further research suggests the slab was once a wall within an apartment complex. There are no other examples of a diary inscribed upon one's living quarters. Second, at least three distinct styles of handwriting are employed on the slab. Note that I do not say there were at least three authors. Careful analysis by my colleague suggests that all the writing was produced by a single paw, though at first glance you would think it must have been entirely separate personalities responsible for each of the remarkably distinct scripts.

I obtained the slab, with much difficulty, from a tar pit. When I cleaned the surface, I was startled to find such a complete specimen of Late-Age New Growl text.

ITEM A: "The Cement Diary of Jacco M. Guus"

The fog that prowls the alleys and crevices of Mist-o'er-Mandrake is sentient. You know this, Jacco. Everyone knows this.

No one talks about it. But you and I talk about it, don't we, Jacco? You trust me. I've gotten you out of every hole you've dug yourself into so far.

Look the other way when the fog wants to show you a secret.

It's best not to admit the neighborhood you live in, if you live outside the upper districts of New Growl. It's best not to admit who you are, if you're not a bourgeois beast, nor a feral one.

Jacco M. Guus, you are neither. You paw your way through a liminal existence. Scrub, rinse, dry. A dishwasher, that's all. Chatter, amble, gesticulate. A late-night comic, every once in a while permitted on stage when the last of the faux-emerald snifters clinked on the drying rack, heralding the end of the dreaded shift.

Blue Font. A smoky jazz lounge. Is the smoke sentient too? You'd think it'd have a hint of spirit, since it spirals from the snouts of thieves, saints, and others who scheme. But, no. Everyone knows the smoke is lifeless. Dry. Bitter. Hollow. It's nothing like the fog.

It can't unfurl itself to reveal a secret you've always known.

"Do you know what they call a crow who never caws?"

"Three marmosets climb into a tavern on 32nd Street. Do you know what they say to the barkeep?"

The worst part about being a late-night comic is that you never know what the laughter is for. It clambers through the smoke, origins unseen. You catch a smirk on a weasel. The bills of robins and blue jays over their steins, they're shaking. But who—or what—is the laughter for?

You spend the night pacing your damp studio, windows shut against the intrusive fog, trying to figure out if the laughter was for or against you, or, perhaps, had nothing to do with you at all.

EMBOSSED IN IVY

Jacco, we gotta move, is what you hear each morning, when the power's out and you're grinding stale coffee beans with mortar and pestle.

(It's not me who says this. It's Another.)

We gotta get outta Mist-o'ver-Mandrake, into a real neighborhood. Do you see the flower pots on the windowsills across the alley? They get replaced, but by whom? There's never a soul on the balconies. The tattered robes on the lines have been there since we moved in. What was that, five months ago? Maybe more?

They're not even putting flowers in the pots at this point.

Little wooden stakes forming crooked pyres. Pyramids of rubble. Skulls so tiny and immaculate they can't be real.

Changed every week. But never an inhabitant or custodian of those old brownstone apartments in sight.

We gotta move, Jacco, we gotta move.

But things could always take a turn, you say.

Something glimmers in the alley behind Blue Font, when your shift is done, when Shagbark has rejected your plea for a spot on stage. The fog unveils a rare coin worth a small fortune. Enough to buy a new corduroy jacket. A red velvet bowler. A shiny cigarette case to keep your punch lines in. To move. Ah, where's the vessel that will transport you to a penthouse in the upper districts!

A talent scout from Mirror Maze—a badger with a blue linen suit and a manicured white stripe between glazed eyes— has wandered inside the lounge, with a sinuous shadow nestled against his haunches. Her stripe, unlike his, is jagged and wild. His laughter pierces the smoke's afterthoughts of afterthoughts. He laughs for you, perhaps.

Yes, it keeps you going, this daydream, though the immaculate skulls in the flower pots grow in number each morning, judging you with vacant sockets that pierce the thin gray curtains.

Things could always take a turn.

What has the fog revealed?

The fear of a closed suitcase. It's always been with you.

A whole life could be inside. In fragments maybe, but a life nonetheless. Clothing, diary, a key to a door which someone will never unlock again. So fragile.

Your life could be snapped up and taken anywhere.

Or, the suitcase could be empty. Oh god, what if it's empty? What if, where the ephemera should be, there's nothing?

The void inside an empty suitcase might be vaster than the void inside your heart. The streetlights buzz unseen behind the fog outside your window—unseen, unimaginable, the stars.

When the fog lifted its skirt this morning, it unveiled a suitcase, abandoned, a solitary symbol nestled between the four cloven hooves of a wrought iron bench.

You snatched it up. So uncharacteristic, cautious mongoose you.

But maybe, Jacco M. Guus, your heart has taken a turn.

Stained in scarlet, embossed with ivy, the suitcase has made your apartment its home. Sullen. Possessive. Inviting. Teasing. The suitcase likes it here. From old magazines cuttings scattered on a creaking coffee table, the suitcase makes a shrine.

Oh Jacco, you shouldn't have snatched it.

Under the roar of the metro you muttered, "It's the right thing to do, after all, to recover what someone else has lost. I'll get it back to them."

We both knew that was a lie.

You didn't even bother to decipher the illegible address.

Had you inspected, you would've seen it wasn't an address at all. No alphabet in New Growl contains such rigid, angular letters.

It's been two weeks since mangy old Shagbark—him of the slick coat and drooping whiskers—has let you on stage.

Not tonight, Jacco, not tonight. It's the girls from Bogtown up next, and then the Restless Prestidigitators. We're full up til 4am. The drinks don't stop being drank. There's all them pots Bollhold used to boil that stew. Next week, little fella, next week. Do yer job like yer doin, and you'll get what's comin.

Next week, next week . . .

But Jacco, the flower pots could be overflowing with skulls by then! But all the suitcases in all the world couldn't pack you up by then. You'll be shredded and spun into a thousand pieces down a million identical alleys if you wait a second longer. The fog of Mist-o'er-Mandrake does not wait for any critter to get their shit together.

Especially not critters like us.

Above the din in your apartment, you hear her voice.

"Jacco, when you gonna tell us what's in that suitcase?"

The skunk has ruby slippers, but she's not wearing them. She made a show of dropping them with a clack-clack on the linoleum foyer when she entered, calling attention to how little she cared if someone (the lynx, if you had to guess) slid them into a leather bag when no one was looking.

Who invited all these others, anyhow? The squirrels have made a mess of the porch, converting flower pots into ashtrays. They must have pranced across the clothes lines to steal them. Oh god, they've sprinkled the skulls with ash, jammed the eye sockets with cigarette filters.

"It's a fine specimen, if a tad sentimental," says Festus Fink, our nearest (in fact, our only) neighbor—the fox gone grey, living on a pension from some municipal post he himself no longer can explain the purpose of. He's chewing his overgrown nails, eyeing the suitcase with something like trepidation, (or envy, I suggest). "I'd say it's ebony from the Isles of Farsight, stained with the blistering ochre of the Ravished Archipelago. But the emerald hue of the ivy, it's unlike anything I've seen. It almost looks... alive. Where in Gaia did you grab it?"

Make something up, Jacco. Make it up fast. C'mon. Are you a maestro of improv, or aren't you? You can't let them get curious. Those weasels drinking all your gin will pry it open if you can't satisfy them.

"New material I'm workin' on."

Good job, Jacco. If there ever was anything in the world that no one could care less about...

But before you can sigh in relief and swig your rhubarb wine, that damn skunk has her charms...

"Oh, let us hear, won't you? I'm so bored. Tell us a joke. Make us laugh, silly mongoose you!"

You would very easily be seduced by the meaningful twitch of that bristly white tail, if it weren't for the menace of the closed suitcase beside you—a mystery that has nested there on your coffee table, amid its garland of yellowed magazine clippings, for seven days, waiting, not caring whether you open it or not. Not caring, but...

Inviting.

The seduction of a closed suitcase has always been with you. This is what the fog revealed.

Maybe you wanted to impress her.

Or maybe you wanted to know.

The diary on the cement slab intrigued me, but I would never have continued my search for Jacco M. Guus had I not, by an extraordinary stroke of luck, stumbled upon the following document, which appears to be the notes of an investigator unlike any we have need for today. I found the document in a dull, rectangular building in which some of the rooms were divided by vertical metal bars, the purpose of which we can only guess.

In this document, I thought perhaps I gleaned a hint of how New Growl met its abrupt end.

ITEM B: "The Investigation Notes"

Incident #	5879-23-4919
Date	REDACTED
Time	REDACTED
Location	427 West Lichenstone Blvd, APT 301 Mist-o'er-Mangrove New Growl
Investigator	Det. Ralys Runstine, Badge #0609
Case Title/Subject	Petty larceny / REDACTED / Missing persons
Synopsis (brief)	Follow-up interview with witness Elizila Mat'aa regarding events in the apartment of Jacco M. Guus.

RR: There's nothing left but cinders and skulls. I need you to take me back to that night. I need you to remember everything you saw. What was a skunk like you doin' in Mist-o'er-Mandrake, anyway?

EM: Can't a girl get out? Can't she go new places now and then?

RR: No one goes to a place like that for an innocent night on the town.

EM: Well... (*laughs*) now you're puttin' words in my mouth.

RR: You were lookin' to pick up spores, weren't you?

EM: Oh please. I can get anything I want in Thistle Town, without ever having to cross a bridge.

RR: Then why that decrepit neighborhood? Why that shabby apartment building? Why that mongoose's place?

EM: Do you have a light?

RR: I don't smoke.

EM: Don't ya keep 'em around for all the pretty minxes you bring in here for questioning?

RR: You've been watching old films.

EM: I like old films. I like the grainy texture. It feels more accurate to the way the world feels. At least... (*her eyes grow distant*

     EMBOSSED IN IVY

and her tail gathers around her ruby slippers, beneath her coat) the way it feels when I'm truly alive.

RR: 'Alive,' huh? That's an interesting choice of words when I'm dealing with a pile of bones and carapaces in a charnel house. Tell me, Ms. Mat'aa, what is it that makes you feel alive?

EM: *(she pulls an ornate matchbox from her breast pocket and strikes up an extra slim cigarette)* Is that what you'd like to know, detective?

RR: I want to know what was in that suitcase.

EM: You think it was a drug—a chemical?

RR: Witnesses saw you with that badger the week prior. We know the suitcase belonged to him. What we don't know is how it ended up with that mongoose. It seems like a strange coincidence, doesn't it? That you would be seen with the badger at Blue Font, his suitcase goes missing, the mongoose gets it, you end up at said mongoose's apartment, the apartment gets torched, and somehow the suitcase goes missing?

EM: Missing? It got burned up with all the rest. Shame, too. It was a beauty.

RR: It wasn't destroyed.

EM: What? *(her eyes widen and her tail tightens like a noose around her slippers)*

RR: What's wrong?

EM: Nothing. Nothing. (*flicks an inordinate amount of ash onto my chaise*) Why are you saying it wasn't destroyed?

RR: Did you see it burn?

EM: No. But that apartment was a downright inferno. There's no way that wooden box could have survived.

RR: But you didn't see it burn.

EM: Has someone else seen it?

RR: Let me ask the questions.

EM: If you tell me, maybe I can help you find it.

RR: You said you'd never seen it until that night.

EM: (*she stands up, looking so frightened I'm worried she'll spray*) If that suitcase is still around, you need to seal it in cement, do you hear me? You need to bury it. Throw it into the ocean, tie it down with chains in the deepest trench. Get rid of it!

RR: Why? What was inside?

EM: Tell me, is there anything growing in the rubble?

RR: A fast-growing weed of some kind. Must be invasive. It made it hard to search the remains at times.

EM: Oh dammit, we didn't close it in time! We didn't close—

     EMBOSSED IN IVY

Unfortunately, the rest of the document had been ripped away.

By this point, after the second uninvited appearance of Jacco M. Guus in my diggings, I initiated my famed endeavor to learn everything about him I could. After a lifetime, this is all I have to show. This letter—unopened—was found inside a cavernous hollow within a petrified sequoia deep within the bay.

ITEM C: "An Unopened Letter"

festus, hope yer safer then me old nayber ole pal.

sorry can't say just where I'm holed up these days. sorry can't get any pounds to ya fer all the trouble I loosed on to ya that nite.

but ya gotta know i'm tryna make it up to all of youse. tryna make sense. it's all I can do

i shoulda known not to trust her. it was her I saw that night at blue font after all, that nite before i snagged the suitcase. she knew. she knew far more than she let on

ah, embossed in ivy!

what a life, what a mess we make just by tryna grab operatunity when it slivers to us unexpcted

shoulda known not to trust a skunk that hangs with a badger in a blue suit

well whut you should know is whut we let loos that nite was only a bigenning, i'm seein now.

cuz ya see every day most my life theres been this Other voice, this other me that speaks to me about what I shoulda an shouldn'ta done. an it was warnin me not to grab that suitcase

but how do ya know what voices to trust and what not?

after all there was voices in the skulls in the flowerpots too, like I told ya, an i was always glad ya didn't stop talkin to me then and there when i told ya the kindsa things they said

remember they said i sure was to die in mist-o'ver-
mangrove?

well they were wrong

everyun, even the voice in my head, was wrong. I cast off that
voice. it's not callin the shots any more

not in that rundown place, no

that's not where i die

then again, I might already be dead, it's hard to say. it's dark
in here and i haven't eaten in weeks, but I'm still not hungry.
there's just enough a gap for me to slip this letter through

sometimes I feel I'm bein carried

sometimes I feel I'm steerin my way to a new nayborhood,
where someun else'l snatch me up, open me up, and take my
place

sometimes I feel I'm growin like never before

let's hope things take another turn

cuz if I ever get outta here, I sure as hell'll have punch line
for ya

if all new growl ain't embossed in ivy by then

     EMBOSSED IN IVY

ACKNOWLEDGMENTS

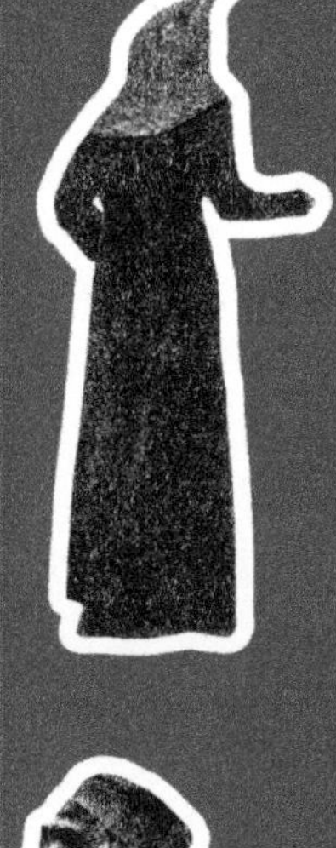

Acknowledgments

I truly cannot express enough gratitude for everyone involved in this project—whether small or large contributions.

To those who listened to me talk and flesh things out, sat beside me while I cut a cat head out, wrote alongside me as I was edited or making graphics or sending emails, thank you. You made every step of this easier, keeping me grounded in the fun bits.

Of course, the hugest thanks goes to the writers who brought *Animal Noir* to life! Thank you Elad, Beth, A.P, M., Megan, Camden, Pen, Phoenix, H.L., Angelique, and Ben. Not only would this not exist without you, there is no way it would be as cohesive and creative with a different group of writers. Your collaboration was a joy to watch, fun to engage with, and even better to read and shape into what it is now.

I appreciate the work you all put in—from concept to writing to chatting on Discord and getting feedback. You're rockstars.

Of course, my love, you must be thanked, if not just for making sure I was fed, watered, and got sunlight during the hours spent editing and making art. Bubee, you make things possible in a very literal way. Also, I love you, and you bring so much light and laughter into my life. Thank you until the end of time.

And, as always, if I missed you, I'm sorry.

If you and I have ever come in contact with one another, if I have ever seen a photo you've taken or street art you painted, if you have ever walked past me or held the door for me, you are probably owed a thank you.

So, thank you, strangers, acquaintances, friends, exes. I'd have fewer stories without you.